ANTI MATTER

KEITH RADMALL

Ordering Information:

Prime Seven Media
518 Landmann St.
Tomah City, WI 54660

Printed in the United States of America

Table of Contents

Just words

Where, when, what, when all there was.

Examples : were taken away, when time as gone by, what is an object when not in the present.

This is as is anti-matter, where everything is not as a form as is., but a form as was.

Perceiving anti-matter is as you think you have it in your hand. But in their reality they have your hand. How far I am going to be able to take this before it dissolves on me I do not know. But in my mind this quest of anti-matter journey is within reach. When something is created in matter time it leaves behind an aurora of what once was. So imagine the image for everything, but then imagine it is for something else. Then we take the parts of everything as singularities and imagine they are something else.

The first step is to find a window to anti-matter space. Anti matter is not the dilapidation of an object because it is or known of no use. Anti-matter is the dilapidation of the parts the human eye does not see. Then forming those particle find into a way of being, for time being then with others as a form of being.

Anti-matter is a mass stratosphere as you might recognise as a galaxy. It is a diversifying of particle compounds. As you might see as a table when it is passed through it is something else. Until it has reason to return to its starting format. It will devise and change many times. Probability with capability of change millions of times over. I have calculations of anti-matter phenomenon. So I need proof before I can verify.

Just words / Part #2

Solids cannot survive in anti-matter space because there is no cell structure. Just the division of all through various cycles of change. That is why no solid as a probability of existence with continuous spacial change.

Anti-matter is not a dido a.k.a. delete. It is a atomized structure that destroys to form again. A.K.A. without change you die from lack of energy. It is this quest I seek to find the entrance to within. To then materialise as one and then be and do as is its way. Then eventually materialising in one of its wonderous beyond. There has to be better than what this place thinks it as to offer. The downfall is there is no knowledge of knowing there is evidence. Calculating about anti-matter format I have decided to go the new world direction. Because unlike the vast knowledge of the known world the findings if any shall be untainted. Compared to the known world. Having set sail in January 1642 from Dunafrie Erie I was surprised how many families were willing to make the perilous journey. I only asked fifteen shilling per family if they could pay. Leaving in the early hours to avoid the approaching British soldiers. Is clear as word of freedom spread it also releases the buzzards. On my journey onboard the Skull Crisp the name of our vessel. I spent most of my time in my cabin figuring my plan of action. Only coming out for fresh air and to stem the hunger. I have decided to do a in depth search of the America's going from north to south.

I will try to create a diaphragm of over lapping degrees, to see if the data connect. To form a directional indicator these are the writings. Emporium : Hello welcome to a space emporium. I would like to introduce you to what I have called a parallax (time lock).

Part one,. As the planet becomes too heavy with an ever growing population and dwindling resources. The planet is getting lighter and with the arborealism which decipher the gravitational requirements. Being less respected the planet is beginning to some people would say encounter stronger rays from the sun, causing changing weather patterns. Others would say causing the planet to race towards the sun.

Part two,. With the planet changing format of resources and weather patterns. Strange experiences such as health problems. The way space sees the planet is causing the vortex to tilt on its axis. Where we can expect stronger voids in time, where spats of suspended animation would take place. Possibly getting lengthy because of unsustainability. Where planets are not what or where they are supposed to be. Universal phenomena appearing more frequently. Where voids a.k.a. worm holes are more common. Eclipses of the sun more common.

Part three,. Where actions of humanity are having a differential effect on everything. So becoming victim of its actions. Trashing the planet, seeing more voids than expected. Putting junk into space. Devastating anomalies on the planet. Strange temperatures in unexpected places, far higher than usual for the season.

In all theorising for the planet I see no survival for it. Except for the changes it make for its self-wellbeing. Compounding the deteriorating factor.

Just words / Part #3

I am about to proceed on my greatest adventure yet. That is to go in search and find anti-matter. After docking in London I collected my trading charters. Then I brought a kaleidoscope which I put in my newly brought back pack. Then returned to port for preparation to set sail for Erie for further cargo.

There I seem to have come upon a time of domestic consequences. Where the locals are in a struggle with British red coats for control of the island. With famine and lawlessness being rampant. I have had a meeting with local dignitaries. Besides the monies for supplies looking as they would be very welcome I have agreed to take as many families as I can to the new world. For the price of fifteen shilling per family.

Word has reached my ears that the British are getting curious as to what I am doing. So on the next gloomy night I have decided to up anchor and try to slip out of port unnoticed.

So with supplies and homesteaders for the new world on board. I was a bit jittery at the number of well-wishers. Which looked like the whole village had turned up to say goodbye. To loved ones and send love and kisses for a good journey.

When the mist rolled in the foot plank was released and the anchor hauled in. There was no incident as the sails were steadily cast. We were out within and at the mercy of the sea for a studious and perilous journey.

To be honest I had no intentions of picking up passengers but just pick up supplies. Most important to me was my journey in search of the unknown, that being anti matter. But starting in depth contaminated Northern hemisphere or starting a new in the Western hemisphere of the new world. A chance of clearer vision was my choosing factor. Once at sea I gave instruction to Bent first mate and retired to my cabin. Leaving him in charge and to give me updates an call me in an emergency.

Just words / Part #4

I have put the thoughts of the Parallax into the back of my mind. But I will use it in my quest with each collective finding I come upon. It is a long shot, it might work or might not. In this day and age if I talked of the way I am thinking, it would be of to the mad house or worse. Especially considering as farfetched my mind was drained. I felt I had slept a week before I felt energy rise in me once more.

Besides the usual sea sickness and varying seas the crossing was uneventful. Except for the birth of a baby girl. Which because of the joy I saw myself having to make sure the crew at best stayed sober. At the dock it was good to see the joyous faces. As each of the families stepped onto the good earth of the new world.

I then spent time explaining the ins and outs of trade to Bent the first mate. Which he already knew by heart I wager. That and probably wanted a stiff drink by the time I was finished. I still wrote it down for him to be sure.

I then like a bolt told him I would be leaving the ship and that he was now captain. Giving him places on a map for good trade. Then I gave the kings charters to him. Then with the rest of the crew we drank ourselves silly celebrating a goodbye and new beginnings. After watching captain Bent set sail in the early hours of November 2nd 1642. I left the dock at Boston and got a room in a lodge.

To make plans for my expedition starting in America.

I knew I was going to have to listen and learn carefully from the Indian tribes. That it was also going to be dangerous. I was hoping the boiling point between the white man and Indians had not boiled over. Because my only hope is what their heart opens up to me.

I needed to learn from the locals how far I could progress in learning from their knowledge. I was going to need supplies, I intended to map my progress, I would log my learning. So I decided to see where my fortune lead me by remaining in town for the winter. While getting a perspective of where I am and how I shall survive my quest.

Just words / Part #5

So now down to business, I know I will not be going anywhere until April or early May. Idiots that think they can will just get caught in the high country. So I will keep with lodgings until it is spring and clear to go. The first thing is to arrange some winter supplies I shall need. So I went to the hardware store to get them. It takes me a few journeys but I eventually obtain what I want for my stay in town. They are one dozen pens, writing paper, tin foods a selection of three each beans, peaches, stew. Then it is a case of making up a list of accompaniments. Two horses, mule, weapons, bed role, grub stake. Now to wait and observe. It is going to be a boring few months. So I will collect knowledge and offer my services if required. Over the next few months I acquaint myself with the locals. Which was another great joy helping new arrivals build homes. Which was no great feat when it was considered as a past time of nearly all the homesteaders. Then I treated myself and bought myself a rifle and a new knife. I figured if someone was going to kill me it was going to come from a knife in the back or a bullet. The next few months were shy on great. Helping others and catching up with the ladies. Over the while there was only one slight mis-hap. When I took a lady to a barn dance where three hoodlums tried to have their way. If it had not been for her generosity I would have killed them. Otherwise I kept myself busy visiting book outlets and the local printers.

To learn about where abouts of different Indian tribes and what was known of this vastly unexplored place.

Then I started making a list of different tribes, expected locations, their spiritual belief, burial rituals, Supplements. Anything I could ascertain for a complete recognition of my quest. But only excepting as a probability because it was not them. I got my supplies together for a six month hike. 3 rifles, 3 hand guns, 500 rounds of ammo, flour, beans, rope, coffee, soap, razor, rain jacket, balm (shaving cream). It is now the middle of April 1643 and I have made arrangements with the bank. I load up my supplies. Taking one last look around I set forth, thinking here goes nothing.

Ghost walk

So I have started my quest it is 10 a.m. April 12th 1643. I am heading northeast towards the most northly fort in America. I have heard that a Cree tribe is camped in the area. I reached the fort on the coast three weeks later. It is a strong fortified fort with a native encampment around the fort entrance. I spend the next while trying to communicate with the Cree tribe. Facts I learn are they call the creator of all Kikei Manito. That all animals have a spirit. The evil spirits are mythological figures that eat their victims—described as monsters. They prey to their spirit. They are a northern tribe. They bury their dead in a blanket of respect and chant songs. An interesting start, now I am going to pack my gear and go to the fort at the tip of lake Sarnia. It took me five weeks to reach the fort and so far the journey has been uneventful. Camping just of track to avoid opportunists. At the fort I learn the tribe is of Mohawk descent. They have an encampment just over the west hill side, and with a few teepees outside the fort. A northern tribe which covers a vast region of northeast America. Their burial rights are to the ground. With a lodge for ten days of celebration. All possessions are given away to prevent further grief. They call the creator of all Tawiskason god of destruction and Okwirasek the god of life creator of things for humanity. A farming people. The men fish and hunt. Cook their food on stone hearths. My next port of call I have intended to be the area of the township of Pennsylvania. Having learnt there are two tribes Shawnee and Cherokee in the area. This part of the journey was eventful. Catching up with a wagon train of settlers. So riding along with them as far as Pennsylvania. I took this point as a chance of learning a white man perspective. Learning that trust between was in short supply. That they thought a Indian uprising was coming. Their understanding of Indian culture was very limited. They segregated Indians from their culture as much as possible. The two tribes lived just south of the fort, south of the township. Shawnee over the hill to the west and the Cherokee to the east in the valley. Both about two miles away. The Shawnee culture existed with the agriculture cycle. The spring bread and planting time dance. The green corn dance when crops ripened. Autumn bread dance to celebrate harvest. They have a proverb a.k.a. golden rule. Do not kill or injure your neighbour. For it is not him you injure, you injure yourself. Known as fierce warriors. Name means southern people. Legend : Spirit Aarka Manetoo gave land to Shawnee.

Ghost walk / Part #2

The Cherokee nation were often used as peacemakers between other tribes. They believe before creation there was empty space. Within the emptiness was a spirit called Kishelamakank who slept a dream which created planet earth. When they die a shallow grave is made lined with bark, grass or plants. To avoid bad dreams tobacco smoke and a wash was performed. Red cedar smoke used to purify a home from tragedy. Four weeks have past and I am looking at a chart to choose my next direction. My next move was to hitch up with a cattle drive. Hiring on as a drover. From Pennsylvania across America to a place called Wyoming. So the next six months I shall not lye were tough going. On our trek we came upon a Sioux encampment. Where cattle was traded to cross their land.

I learned that they were a warrior tribe and an act of bravery gave them the right to wear the bear claw necklace. They called the creator Wakan Tanka. Their religion is to communicate with spirits through dance and music. They live their lives on the prairie land.

After a gruelling trek we finally reached Wyoming-fort town. Where the cattle were a very welcomed commodity. After getting paid off I got lodgings for a well earnt rest.

While about I learnt that just south of town about one and half miles out was a Cheyenne tribe. Half way out was a trading post so loading goods I went to learn of the Cheyenne peoples. While trading of tobacco, salt beef, a couple of weapons. This is what I learnt.

They called the creator M,heo,o They buried their dead in trees, when no trees constructed a platform 8' to 10' high. Skilled warriors of horseback. A trading tribe. They farmed, hunted, made pottery, gathered wild rice.

After getting back to town with Neddy who looked well happy to be rid of the rubbish. I thought what more excitement await me.

When my stay in town comes to a end I have decided to travel down the west coast. So a plan of action and manipulation had to be carefully put together. I remained in town until spring an did so by getting lodgings in a boarding house. I paid my dues in full up to April. So when spring came I intended to travel the coast to California. The town was a hub for supplies to be taken along the west coast. So I got myself work in one of the town forges. Making knives, axes, shovels, wheels for wagons, shoes for horses etc. It was hard work but the finished product made it well worth it. During the passing months I met a trader who like myself was stuck in town. Because of the cold season where -20 was much the normal. But come spring he would take trade wagons down the coast to Portland town. So we struck up a deal that I paid for a shipment. Then on arrival I got more than I paid for the goods. Though hunting was a plenty in the west they still needed clothing, implements, stationary, cooking utensils, and other food products. He had been trading for some ten years.

Ghost walk / Part #3

So I did a deal in which I gave financial support an double my money. So come spring I bought a wagon supply of grain, soya beans, dried peas, wheat, seedlings and eight goats.

Then in April 1644 we made tracks for Portland township deep in the mountains. It was quiet the nerve raking journey. Where travelling over treacherous mountains we reached town. Where the trader was as good as his word. Then after five days I caught a wagon train over the perilous pass that seemed to go up and up into California. It was very satisfying to think we had succeeded in such a trek. California was a green landscape of rolling hills and woodland. With a beautiful golden sanded coastline.

Not until I reached southern California did I come upon a tribe of Mojave Indians. I had to be very coy with the knowledge that hostilities between Indians and settlers was getting very tense. I traded a deal for direction to spirit in the sky. They were known for dreams and visions. Which they considered a source of knowledge. They farmed, fished, hunted and gathered wild plants. Meaning of word Mojave, lived by the water.

Then travelling alone I reached Texas coming across various towns with Apache Indians in.

A Indian native to southwest America. Meaning of word Apache is enemy. A nomadic people. Used horses for main stay of travel. Their beliefs are in nature and the supernatural.

I had one more interest in the evolvement of America. That being the Indians of the swamp land of southeast America. So I am heading into the very humid swamp land. It is a rugged land and if you think the desert land of Texas was hot. This humid sticky land leaves it standing.

It has been four months and I am going to meet up with the Seminole Indians. Who led by an interpreter has got me a pow wow with the chief. We share a greeting and I offer an assortment of gifts. Mirror, tobacco, knife, jewels, as a thank you for seeing me. We smoked a peace pipe. Then I started with the questions.

I learnt there religious dance the stomp was a colourful spectacle. They did the green corn ceremony. Tribal name meaning, wild one. To be close to them but not interfere in their culture sent a strange sensation through me.

Also on my travels I learnt about Totem poles.

Which were carved from wood. Symbolise ancestors, cultural beliefs, commemorate ancestors, clan linages, notable events.

Then there was the peace pipe smoked before ironing out differences. Now it was time to travel to the port of Tampa and cross the Gulf of Mexico into Mexico. Which would give me time to compile what information I had collected together so far. At Tampa I decided to rest up look for work for a couple of months then sail to Mexico.

Ghost walk / Part #4

I have spent the past three weeks trekking to Tampa. It is a up and coming town. Which seems to be a magnet for trade along the coast and across the Gulf to Mexico. But for now I have got myself lodgings in Tampa for a week. So I can try to make sense of the information I have learnt. Anti-matter is a form of is not but possesses a existence. A unprobeable understanding by humanity. Because it does not give or expect from a human belief. Your probably wondering why I took the improbable trek around the new world. Well I did so because it is probably the only place on the planet earth where facts are not distorted through time. So much as not to have distorted the whole truth. I have placed all the information I have gathered on my journey in front of me. Now I am putting wording into context to try to read them out.

Apache : meaning enemy, nomadic farmers, horses for travel.
Seminole : meaning wild one, religious stomp dance, green corn ceremony.
Cherokee : peace keepers amongst tribes, empty space before creation-where spirit slept and dreamt creation on earth, Dead buried in shallow grave lined with tree branches or plants, Good wash and tobacco smoke keep bad spirit away, red cedar wood used to purify home.
Sioux : warrior tribe, ware bear necklace for bravery, connect with spirit through dance and music.
Cheyenne : buried dead in trees, warrior of horseback, traders, farmers, hunters, pottery makers, gathered wild rice.

Cree : all animals have spirit, evil spirits ate their victims, buried their dead in a blanket of respect and chanted songs.

Mohawk : have a god of destruction and a god of peace, bury dead in ground, all possessions given away to prevent further grief, farmers, fish, hunt, use stone hearth for cooking.

Shawnee : meaning southern people, known as fierce warriors, existence in agriculture cycle, believe spirit gave land to their people. They were farmers, warriors, hunters. The spirit was a mixture of beliefs. With peace and destruction being clearly intertwined but different. The meaning of the tribal name seemed significant. Where with Apache-enemy, nothing to be found here.

Shawnee-southern people, drawing me southward.

Seminole-wild one, a trek meaning be weary at all times.

Cherokee : peace keeper, empty space, dream creation.

I have got the inclination I am on the right trek. But I have the wrong end of the stick.

If their beliefs are in agriculture. Then they are warriors to protect their beliefs. Then their name is a slant on what I seek. It is good to know I have sense I am on the right path.

They are truly a warrior race so I do not need the parallax yet because I sense them.

How strange it is to have a read on the future that does not exist yet.

Unfolding

It is early dawn and the ship as cast off. From finding the entrance way to anti-matter I hope now I can learn another clue from the natives of Central America. There bypass and enter into its wonderful being. Ten weeks later I have arrived in eastern Mexico after working my passage on the trading ship. Around the coast of America and down the east coast of Mexico. It looks a bit of a ramshackle of a country where people are trying to eek a living anyway they can. It is easy to see why Mexico will struggle to be recognised. The French and Spanish have divided the country into fifteen or more territories. With both vying for and draining the resources out of the country as meaningful and as quickly as they can. Starvation and poverty is quickly becoming the normal. Except for the privileged few and the military which take as much as they want when they want it. It is a terrible situation for the Mayan Indians. While under the banner of war the military is exterminating the Mayans wherever possible. With vast treasures being taken in the guise of genocide.

I have been fortunate to gain an audience with the last Mayan emperor, Cantica. His first words to me were Ba-Tak-Ua. Then dipping his finger in red paint from eye to eye around my chin he did make a red marking. Then dipping another finger in white paint he did make a cross between my eyes.

I spent the next day's learning about the crumbling and soon to be extinct Mayan empire. Their empire extended from Mexico to the southern states of Central America. They prayed to the sun god, they created their own calendar, they built pyramid temples, noted for mathematics and astronomy. They had a fascination for gold using it to adorn their surroundings. They used glyphs representing figures and meaning.

I have kept the markings painted on my face and have been to see a soothsayer who explains it is the mark of death. Which explains the strange looks I have gotten.

I am now descending into silent mode to bury the heartache. To reach the boarder I have gained a horse and mule camping as I go. Sticking to the trails as I cross the thick forest across the coastline to enter into South America. Following the directional findings of America and the learning in Central America. I am hoping to connect an divulge the values of my findings in South America.

I am lost in sweat and the Arora of disorder, but my senses have come to my aid. That there is a clear finding to behold. But I have to gain understanding, then direction to find.

Plagiarism

I have just crossed the Mericano frontier into South America. To be honest I do not feel so good. I think all this do da travel has got to me. I am with a group of Paw Indians who are starting to their village, I hope I can last. But a week's journey feeling I can last about a day. I hope they can come up with a miracle cure.

Anyway day two my temperature is in the stratosphere. They are discussing what to make with me. It is they said day four and I am feeling like heck. As the fever brakes on day six all I want to do is thank them. With Tagua, I think that was right. I am now crawling along with them. It is day nine and I feel like a feather brain. But good news we reach their village tomorrow and they say I can rest and camp out. Check if I am still all together.

Well I have set up camp and got me some peyote. Got myself three heads so one of them should fit okay right. It has been fourteen days now and have decided to avoid any more peyote. I have been eating what they gave me which is okay I think, I feel better anyway. Thinking more me I cannot thank them enough so my supplies look like a British prison menu for pirates. But there clean if that mean anything., I hope not I have learnt that the Incas in the Andes mountains is about a seven day journey. Fourteen for me so they have offered me a guide. So now I have no compass. So after saying goodbye all morning. I am stuffed with a market place to make common market jealous. So loaded up with three jars of Peyote and three bags of Peyote. We then set off for the sun temple of the Inca. After twelve gruelling days of seeing forest leaves that looked like butterflies and insects that looked like armies of angles. I was happy to reach the outskirts of the Andes mountains. The guides then left and went on their way to sell their trade goods. Just outside the village town of Lima I set up camp. Brought a supply of stapples and fresh water. Then for the next eight days I was in and out of consciousness. Like receding down a dark tunnel, being ripped apart by demons, awakening in hot and cold sweats. Seeing small creatures shred my skin apart alive, having terrifying thoughts from just thinking.

Then on the ninth day I felt excellent full of energy and refreshed.

I contacted a Oracle in town and when I mentioned Haboona she seemed to be the only one that did not shy away. She told me great mystic so I should consult the Sharma up the mountain. So the following morning I climbed the mountain. Eleven hours later I was wacked. But sure enough there was the Inca medicine doctor chanting away. Waiting until we had eye contact saying sorry to interrupt but I seek your guidance. I said I am in search of the passage way to Haboona. The Sharma said you must tread far beyond to the land of the sun rise. There seek the all seeing eye but remember words are not all you shall behold.

I thanked him for his wisdom and left three marigold fruits and a jar of water. After journeying back to town I suddenly remembered. I did not ask what people I seek.

So I visited the oracle and she said, the land of the sun of the Aztec people. I thanked her leaving another two bits.

Back at camp thinking how to get there was my next thought.

Istoricisum

I am now searching for a way to complete a vast trek to the south of the continent. There is a trader looking for gun bearers and cargo hands to cross with a vast cargo. The cargo contains different metals liquors, precious metals and ornaments. So I have found a way to reach my destiny and get paid. As we are not leaving for a month I have got myself a job in a bar to smarten myself up. So here comes the day of departure. I have prepared as well as I can with getting food stocks, clothes and implements for survival together. The less I have to ask for, the more I receive at finish of expedition. It is a tough trek for the first part of journey over mountains and through rocky desert terrain for seven hundred miles. Then the journey changes to thick forest along hardly recognisable tracks. But the wagons were sturdy and any break downs. Mother nature could take care off. We ate and hunted for food on the way, the home blended grog was not bad either. It helped pass the day away getting over our sore head. After four months and ten days we arrived in the flamboyant and mad city of Rio de Janeiro. If hell had a name this was it. With the arrival of the Portuguese clashes with the Indians were numerous. They had gone mad for the gold and artifacts which were everywhere. People were being hacked and gutted for minor infringements. The empire of the Aztec Indian was disappearing quickly. While living in a tavern of the Portuguese fortification. I sort out the Indian natives that would speak to me. At the mention of anti-matter. They were quick to say no Habooji here. With sentences such as. You find you die, you see you die, to evil no find. But searching in the city I learned of a Aztec Sharma, warning of the end. So I found someone to take me to his village which was located twelve miles out of town. So come dark we slip past the guards on the roads and headed towards the village. When there I thought I had been welcomed to a party in hell. There were heads on sticks, body parts in cauldrons, weird creatures and snakes sleeking around. Food alive and dead was stuffed on the tables. The women did not look bad either. I was introduced to the Sharma named Cotti medicine doctor and gave him a gift of a kaleidoscope looking glass. I told him where I had come from and how I had found him. Then I said I was looking for Habooji. He then gave me a beaker of grog which sent me loopy. Then went on to say, out far beyond where the other is all. No one speak because no one know. It is vast and its mind is vaster.

Written deep in the forest over the great sun are the words of direction. Beyond the sun, where is the sun is what you seek ! But beware find another then you can find no more. For the rest of the night I drank, I ate, I kissed. I do not know what I was doing trying to explain to the guards except trying to explain why I was on a cart horse having lost my guide. The next day I sort out my guide and gave him one-hundred bits.

De-sypheratic

So far after a rest in Rio de Janeiro, Brazil I have now decided to make a chance move out of this horror story I have been entrenched in. I have decided to try to get work with either the trade wagons or trade ships. Down the coast to Buenos Aires, Argentina. Where I can make contact with best vision I can see, search to find. I have discovered that the wagon trains are basically thugs. That rob and kill to increase their reward upon reaching their destination. So I have no qualms about sticking at my job at the bar until I can find a trade ship.

It has now been eight months and the ship Deablo Toarno as offered me work for the next six weeks. For the journey to Bueno -----

The journey was rough and we made four stops loading and unloading trade goods.

The only way to diversify substance for the influx of Europeans. Mainly Spanish, Italian and Portuguese merchants a.k.a. dealers, treasure seekers, refugees. I have now reached Buenos Aires and departed company with my sailing comrades. Buenos Aires is a very important point of execution and outlying Spanish trade in South America. So it is as secure as can be expected for the area. I have got a room at the Inn and after resting for two weeks obtained work on a farm (it is killing me) but a good after effect.

I am now in the process of trying to connect the parallax reader. If it works I shall be out of this world. I have now made a decipher reader out of my findings from central and south America. Now I have deciphered everything I can. From the sense of go from the north to the south, to what is deniable of fake belief to sense of truth in Central and South America. Now everything depends on my findings with the parallax reader.

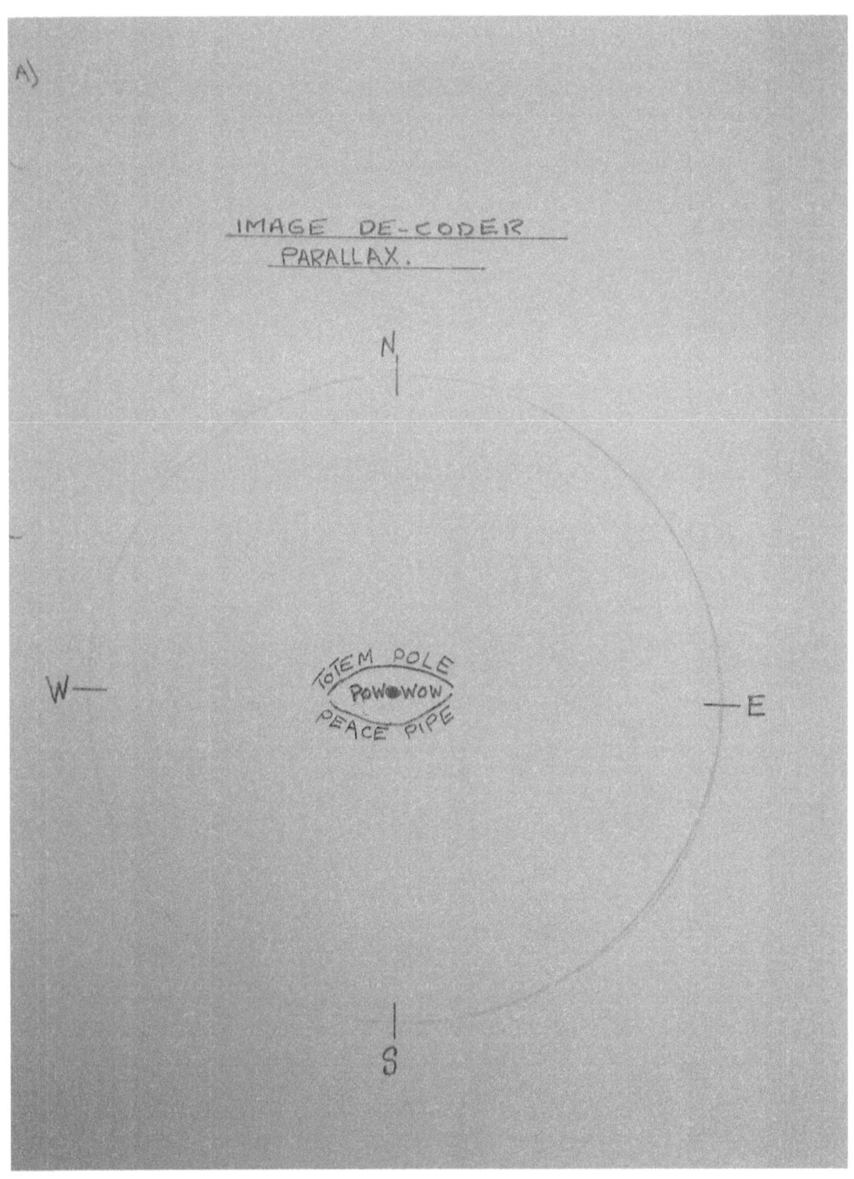
IMAGE DE-CODER
PARALLAX.
N
W
E
S
TOTEM POLE
POW WOW
PEACE PIPE

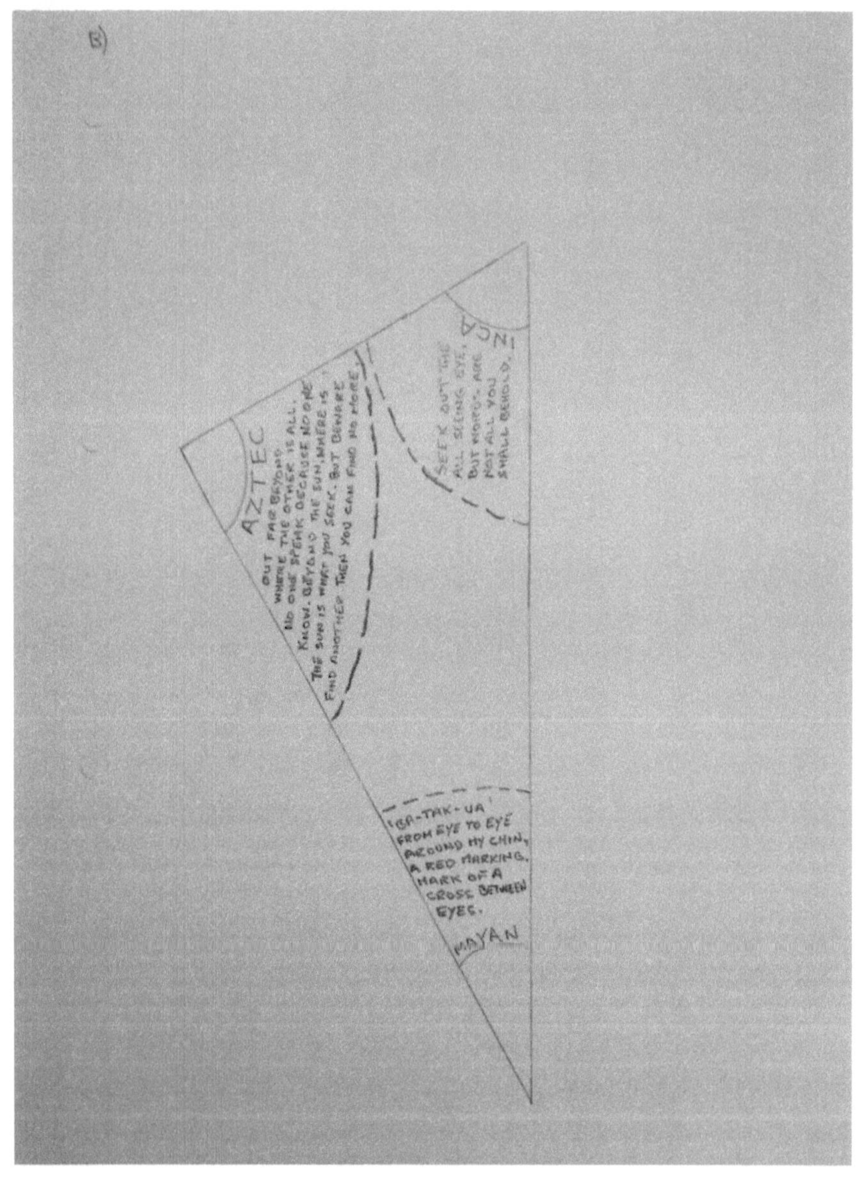

AZTEC
OUT FAR BEYOND
WHERE THE OTHER IS ALL,
NO ONE SPEAK BECAUSE NO ONE
KNOW. BEYOND THE SUN, WHERE IS
THE SUN IS WHAT YOU SEEK. BUT BEWARE
FIND ANOTHER THEN YOU CAN FIND NO MORE.

INCA
SEEK OUT THE
ALL SEEING EYE,
BUT NOTCH ARE
NOT ALL YOU
SHALL BEHOLD.

'BA-TAK-UA'
FROM EYE TO EYE
AROUND MY CHIN,
A RED MARKING.
MARK OF A
CROSS BETWEEN
EYES.

MAYAN

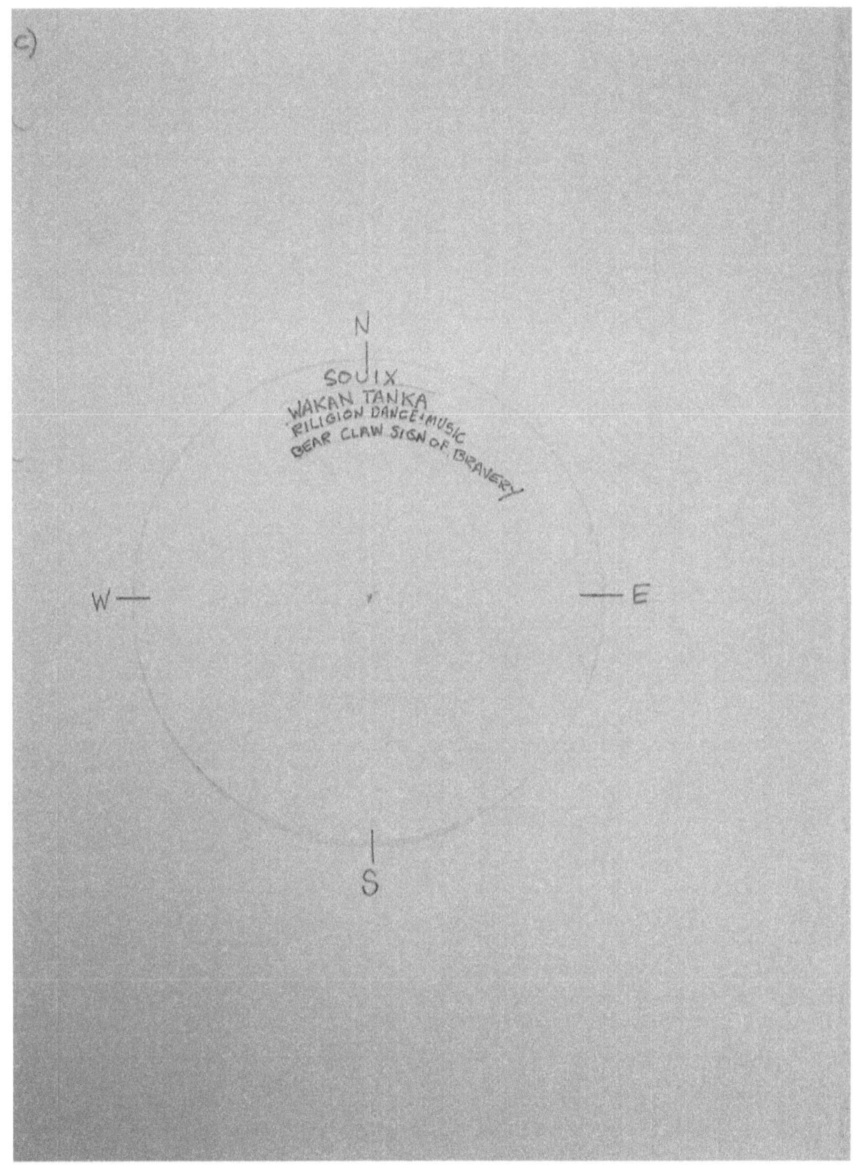
c)
N
SOUIX
WAKAN TANKA
RILIGION DANCE&MUSIC
BEAR CLAW SIGN OF BRAVERY
W
E
S

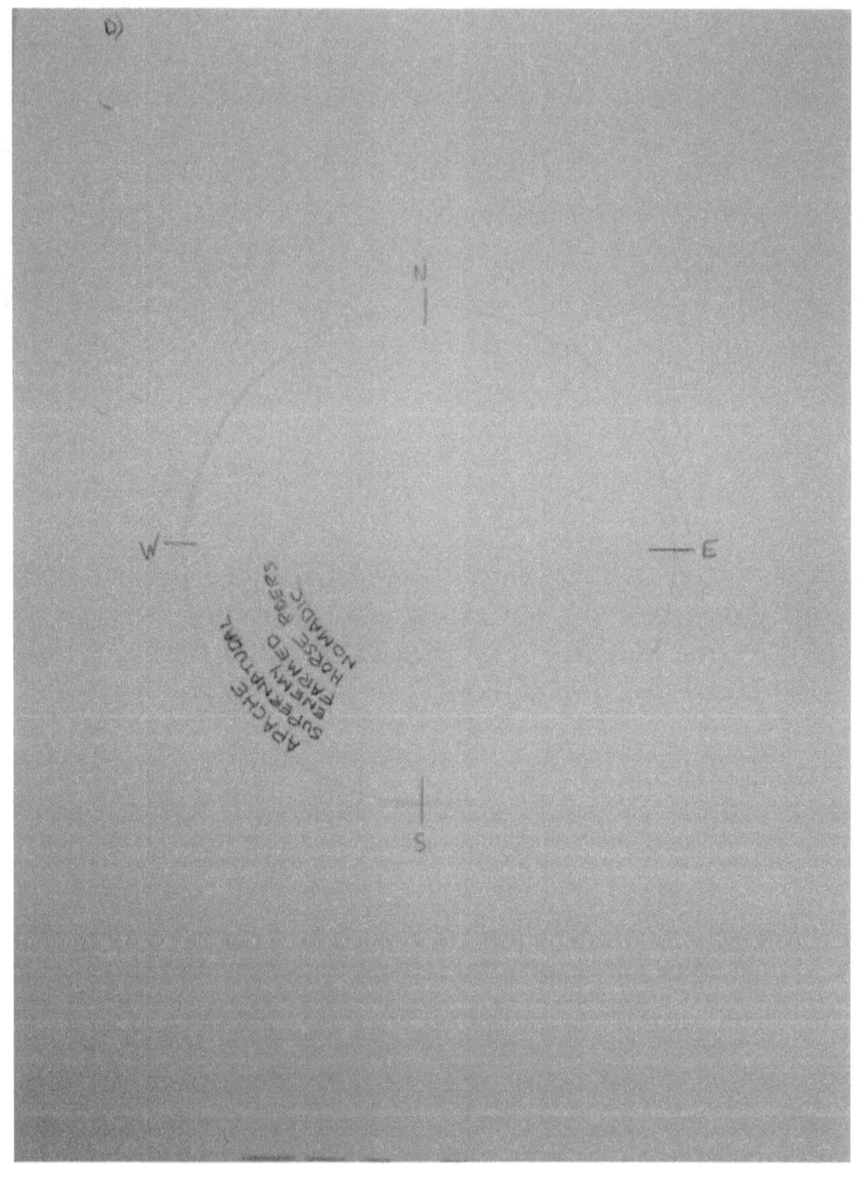

N
W
E
S
APACHE
SUPERNATURAL
ENEMY
FARMED
HORSE
NOMADIC POETS

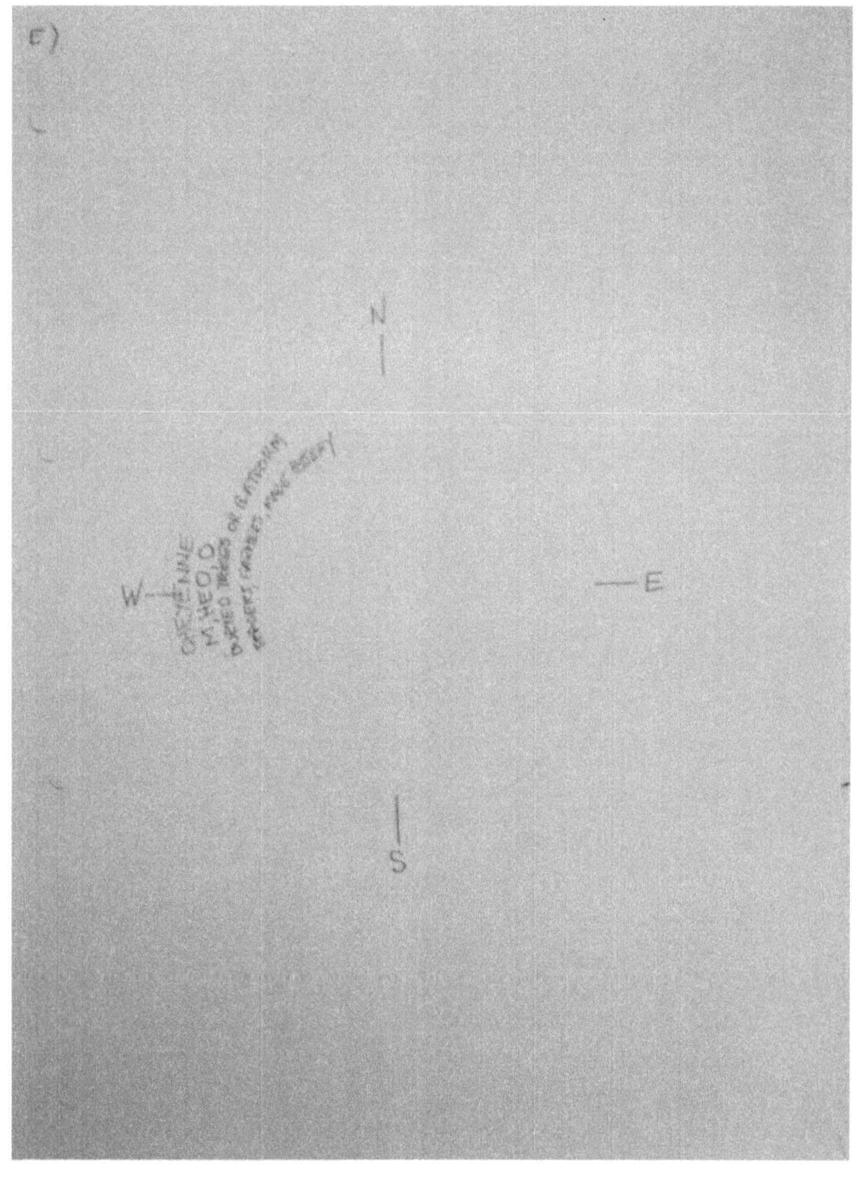

E)
N
W
E
S

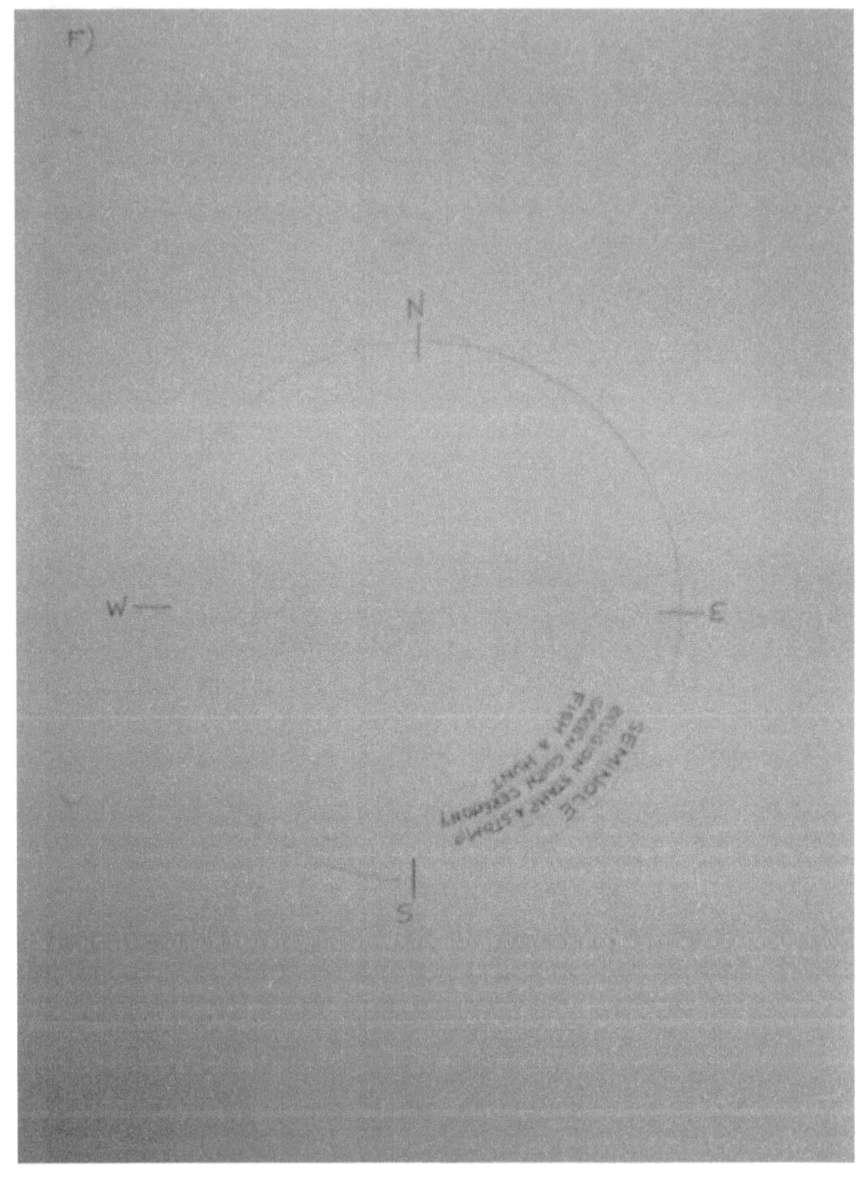
F)
N
W
E
S
SEMINOLE
BROKEN START CEREMONY
PICK A POINT

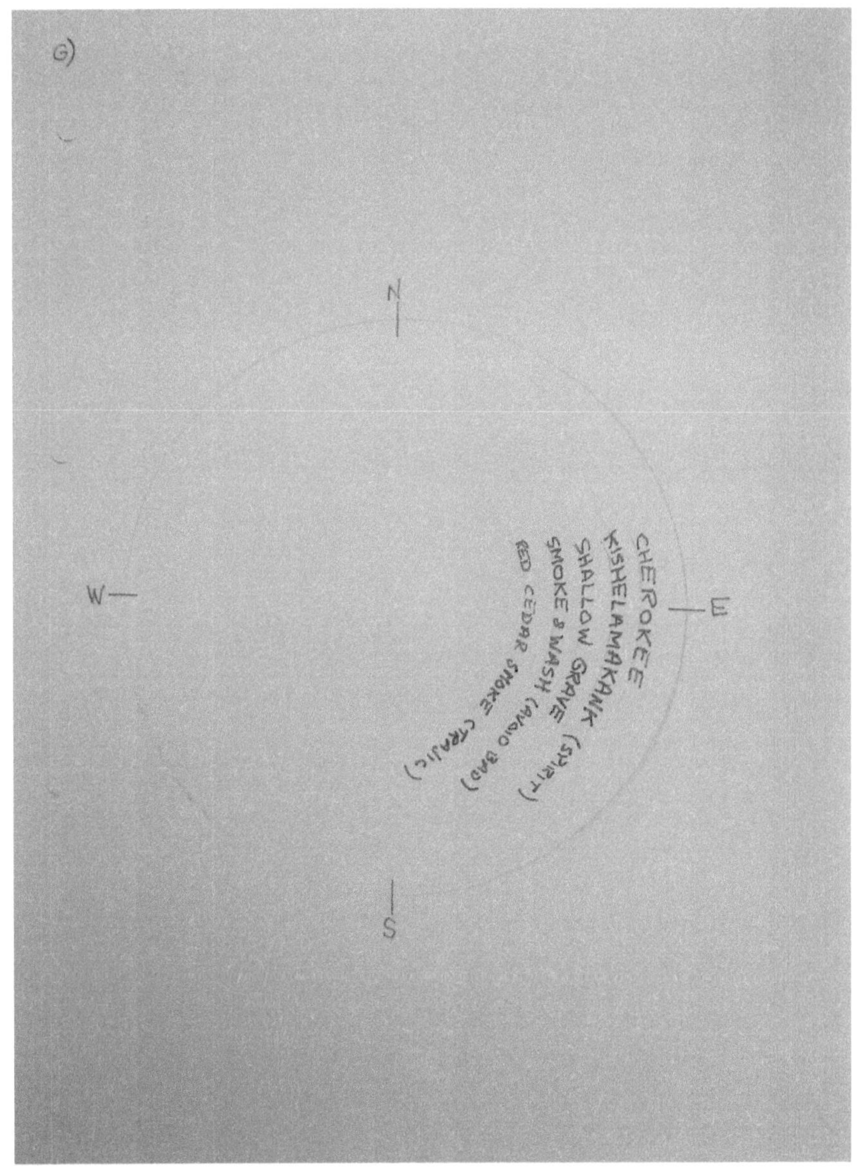

G)
N
E
S
W
CHEROKEE
KISHELAMAKANK (SPIRIT)
SHALLOW GRAVE
SMOKE & WASH (AVOID BAD)
RED CEDAR SMOKE (TRAJIC)

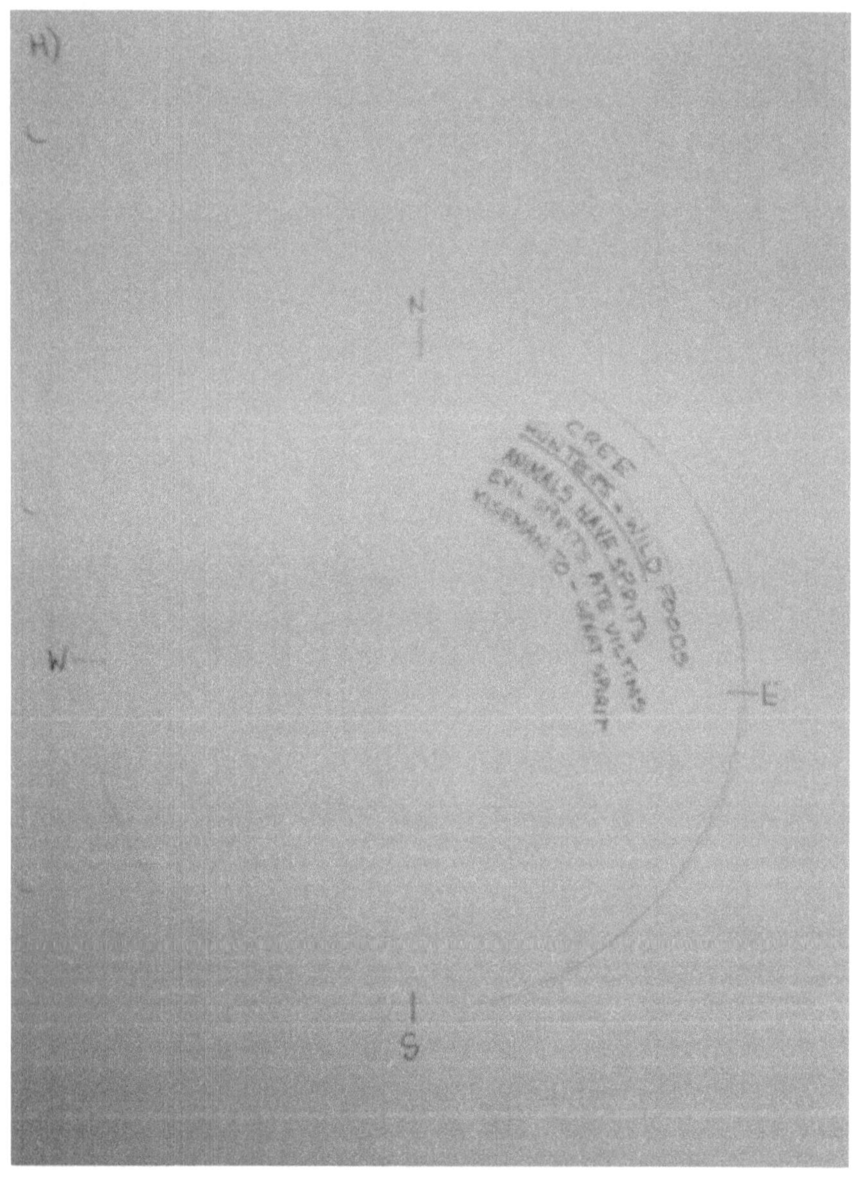
H)
N
W
E
S
CREE
HUNTERS - WILD FOODS
ANIMALS HAVE SPIRITS
EVIL SPIRITS ATE VICTIMS
KISEMAN-TO - GREAT SPIRIT

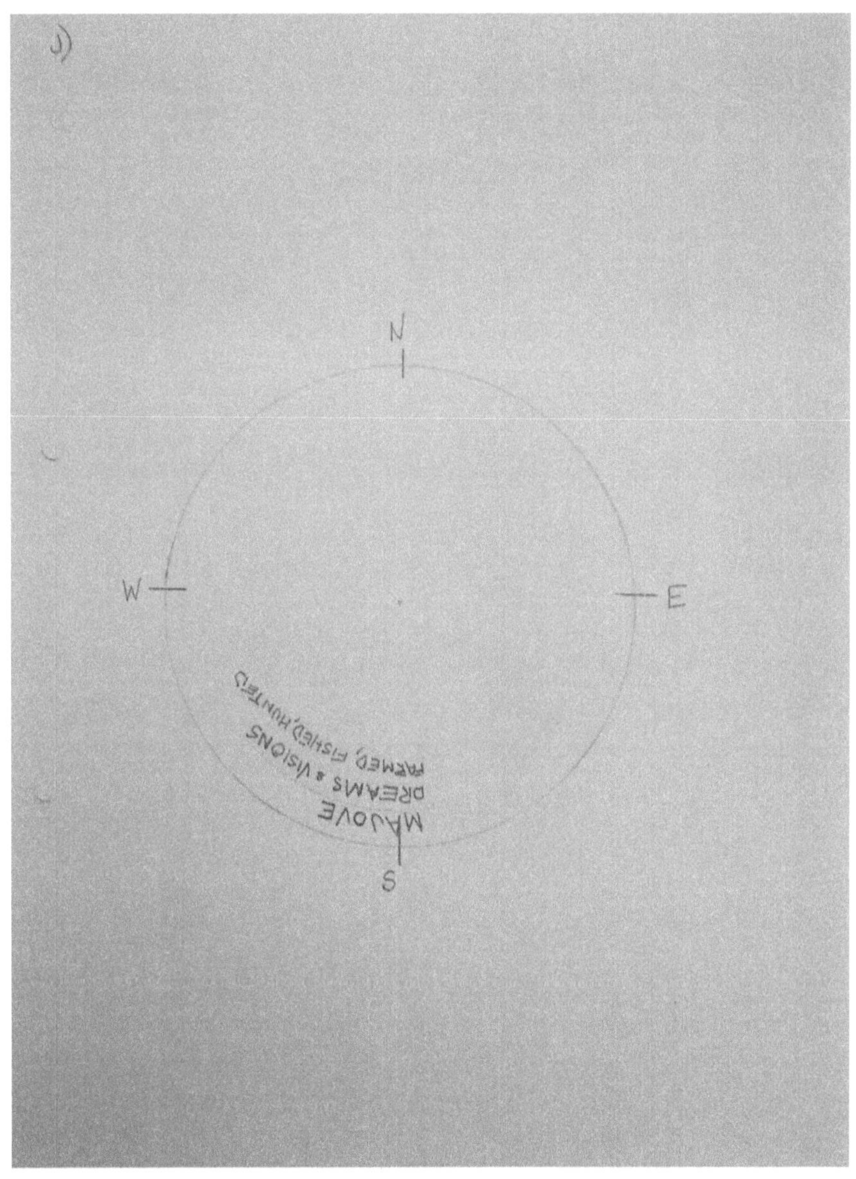

N
E
S
W
MAJOVE
DREAMS & VISIONS
FARMED, FISHED, HUNTED

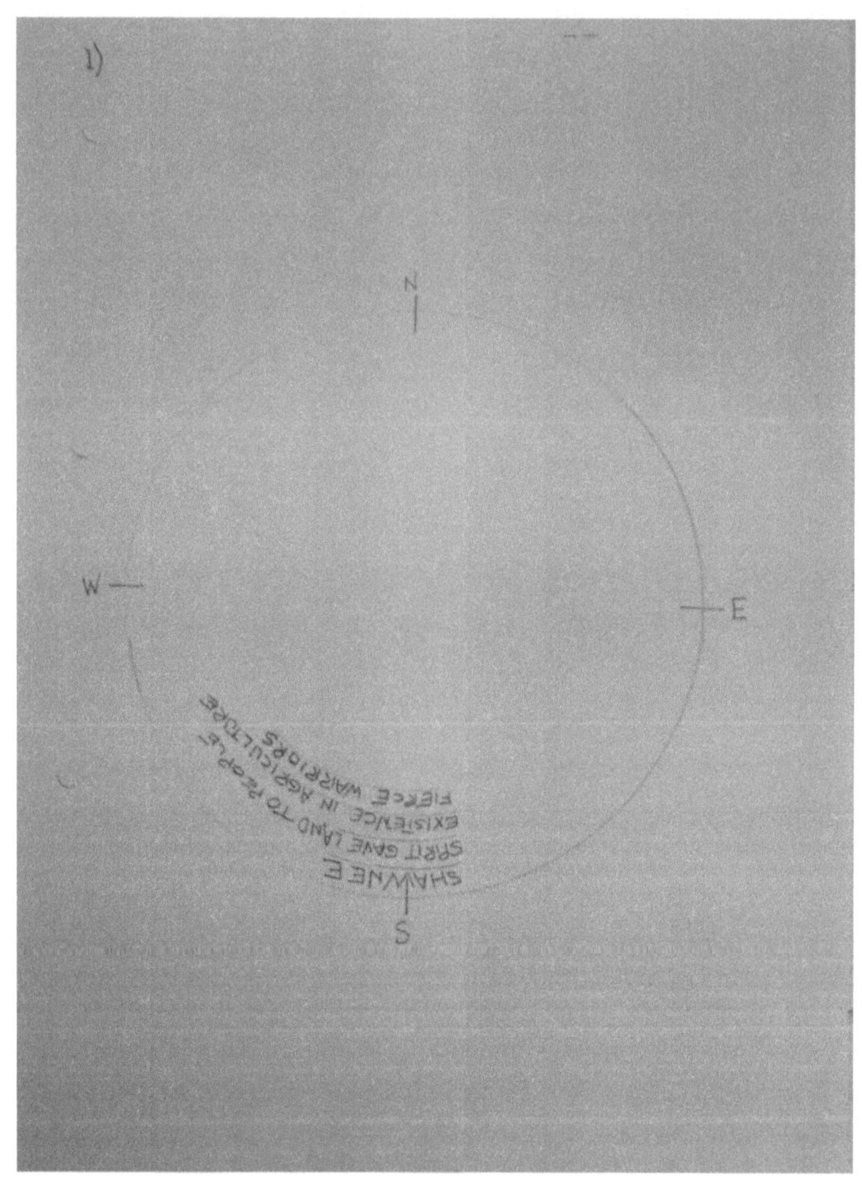
1)
N
W
E
S
SHAWNEE
SPRIT GAVE LAND TO PEOPLE
EXISTENCE IN AGRICULTURE
FIERCE WARRIORS

Walkling

I am stuck in my room, sitting at a table with all the information I have gathered before me.

It is there staring me in the face telling me what to do. Now is the time where everything I have done shall either become a failure or I have a future to look forward to. I have configured how I shall start and finish this trip. When it is to it was, all I have to do is find the entrance way.

I have started to try and read the Parallax and then the more I read the more convinced I become I am in the right area and on the right track. I have one intention now and that is to read the parallax and decipher the co-ordinance as best I can. I have learnt that a medicine man at the village of Jabolla just across the border from Bueno in Rio has what I have referred to as deep medication. So fail or succeed that shall be the place of my decent into another realm. Where thought, bravery and belief shall be my guide.

I want a clear space of mind once I leave, so I am going to configure all the information I have gathered.

Information so far as been sending me southward. That purity has a significance with the other side. That all as a spirit and it as meaning. So bravery must be synthesized to understand the passage as you get used to the surroundings and that no divergence from the trek must be taken. So clear of heart, clear of mind will be the first thought. Then what is once was my last thought. Where within I shall be with and a new beginning at an end shall be a new quest.

Potoniclismic

I have met-up with a Indian named Doinic, who is a trader that trades between villages.

I have fed him enough sangria drink and gold that he has said I can join him as far as the village of Jabolla. So I have got my gear together for what I imagine shall be an exciting journey. We are on the outskirts of town leaving before dawn to avoid the Spanish soldiers. It is a group of seven of us with eight mules and four carts. It is amazing how they know where they are going. Except for the villages the trail looks like thick forest and brush to me. After an epic three and half months the pack train reaches Jabolla. Then I thanked the good Indian and his friends saying good bye in a wild party. You can guess the rest, my hangover is that big. I have been given a hut and spent the day making it look good as if I am going to stay. I guess my Indian friend as explained that I am a nice guy. I have slept for two days, said my good byes and made arrangements to speak with the medicine man.

The Sharma has agreed to on the full sun and half-moon to see and give me the medicine. So on the fourth day in the village I climbed the rock face to the cave of the medicine man. We talked and I explained that I seek haboona and had read signs leading me to his being. I gave the music box and the parallax that I bought in London to him. Saying anything else I had would be free to take. Then he went to give me the liquid potion. Saying when I drink I must drink until it is all gone. Then his face looked anxious so I told him I carry the face of death. Then the tension left him as he gave me the clay jar. I went to the hut and decided when the moon came up I would be gone. That evening sitting down cross legged I cleared my mind.

Placing the clay jar with the potion in to my right side. I then thought what was is and clearing my mind picked up the jar and drank it whole.

Then everything started to fade into a oblivion of emptiness. Then I was gone having entered into a being of nothingness. Where only thinking now I had passed a vast void. Into another dimension of the spirit world of anti-matter. My body had crumbled into non-existence because I had reached my destiny.

Upalossuer

As the mind explodes there is a moment of searing pain. With whatever you think will not recede. Its agonising throbbing, crunching, cave-in effect. The eyes are red getting smaller tunnel vision. To the point of oblivion of burning pain. You have entered a point of a never ending nightmare. The darkness descends upon your being. You then slowly open your eyes as if you have a sense you have been on a journey. But you are at exactly the same place and position you were in when you started the decent. You brush your hands calmly over yourself to insure that you are real. You stand up or move but sense something is not normal. Everything around you begins to look like a melting effect. You sense you are about to fall over and fall into the position you rose from, going into a deep long sleep. When you awaken you cannot remember anything. Except you were on a strange fantastic journey.

Going about what you were doing as if nothing has happened. Slowly forgetting your inquisitive mind. Of what might and might not of happened. Getting up you feel groggy and look outside. Where there is a storm going on like no other. The wind is howling, the tree branches are swaying. Whatever is not tied down is flying in the breeze along with broken branches. You are thankful to be inside, then contemplate what to do.

As time ticks by a new life form has made itself present. Showing its dominance and thinking what to do with what it as found.

Well heck ! the weather is the thought. I cannot do anything with myself. Whereas the planet rising from the dead because of the mighty coronavirus impact. It is thinking what to do with the stiff and what to make of the place.

Spheretic

In the sphere of anti-matter in the eyes of the fact of the movement of a is not. It moves in two motions fast and quick. Their mind is a absorbing factual entity. There was, there is, then the next. They have no sense of smell because everything is a entity of one. Meaning something is equal to nothing. To be devisable everything is a quantity of vision. There to it the atmosphere they dwell in everything with different the only other part.

They move in a transendal movement of partial divide. Anything in the motion divide as no meaning. So they only sense when all before it is a part of sight. The moment of change is when quality of one becomes more or quality of more. Becomes one because it as become more of another number of parts.

This transition of existence lasts as long as the thought of the movement is there being that shows to them as another point of view. It is a vast divide that never stops reshaping to expansion. Only another one of another kind that is not them evolving shows something else exists. They are a thought provoking existence that as evolved as one hand does one thing, then the other hand does another.

All connected through different movements created with mind thoughts. There showing with many it always has a one way purpose. That is to share with as is one.

There moment of aberration is creation of there long forgotten eclipse of the beginning. Then there one heartbreak can be when a thought of return leaves them empty.

It is a vast entourage of want that divides to give a non-existing motion of way. There is never no thinking of horror. It is just a thought of what is there to view because is not.

It is not possible to say where they would go in the outer inner world. Because as one is there destiny awaits. The motion of truth is non-existent. Because it is not a form of anti-matter.

Hope devisable by one to their outer world is there motivation destiny. Do they meet in the afterlife. When caring sharing in a lost changing giving entity. I imagine they meet but do not know how long that before past time span is. They just have an inclination that they were destined. Where anti-matter rises to its fore. How many differences do they behold before. Then the inclination becomes plural.

It is a vast murky place of being of dark colouring surroundings. Colours of brightness are a after effect. There is a sense of foreboding in the atmosphere., where ferocity accumulates, it is a hair line stability. Motion sense is all only nothing until again it is part of past, present and future. Because its sense is not until it is. It has a sun of a speckle of white, their teeth glitter like sense of purpose of whiteness shining like diamonds. Causing with touch a base line effect. Where you as you blink, it is to late it as formed. Try it-you are-you are not, it is you are.

Calamatosous

The inauguration of sound in anti-matter is just a factor of noise. As when a breath is taken it is like an amalgamation of all which creates a whirlwind effect.

Like when you see a change of one to see becomes another part of it. The screeching effect is the devisable of motion from a part to another being. Where you have had mass change such as quack effect or eruption. It is the movement of one mass form to another. Creating a dispersible effect of destructive magnitude. Rushing effect of movement can do this in the way as it the wind wave hit a solid change to a mountain side appearance.

Creating a shattering wind sound effect.

When water appearance of rises giving an appearance of many differences as it change. Showing a desert like appearance of where it once was. But is a mass of what appears as gue. In it is an accumulation of the differences it is able to appear as simultaneously. Noise, sound, echo it is all only a part caused by the sense of movement of the spiralling to change of the anti-matter.

The eye of proportion is divide for all, with every change in the metabolic structure acquiring another view of what is another volume of view. There is no divide in the aquirement and expansion. It is only what it was is. Others are just a matter of fact.

Rareisaty

This story is an example of very rare anti-matter.

While traveling in the pacific raiding ships coming out of the east-indies blockade. The captain of the Mary Celeste decided to run the European blockade, to reach a place called Japan. A very mysterious place, with little known about it in the west. The captain had learnt that to obtain a sword of magnificence. He would have to find a Japanese sword maker. Speaking to his second it was decided to make a brake when the stars were bright in the sky and the breeze was South easterly.

When the right time arose, pushing through the Jawa straight the plan worked perfectly. With the two Portuguese and the French man o, war having to hold back, looking to find direction. The enemy was easily lost in the murky mist heading towards dawn.

Reaching the shores of Japan and docking at a port called Habibo. The captain and Jack Leftee, (He was called that because he was never where he was supposed to be) went off to see a sword maker named Ikado Sachawizo. Leaving instructions to barter and stock up on food and water and to protect the ship. With the reminder that someone had to be sober to watch over the ship.

After a twenty-mile journey they reached the home of the sword maker. Telling of their situation the sword maker said seven weeks. So, the captain said I shall return in nine weeks. Here is twenty-five pieces of eight, with another twenty-five with completion of scabbard & sword. Thereafter between not much was remembered except alcohol, women and the word more! At the end of the nine weeks Jack and the captain returned to the home of Ikado the sword maker. Paying the final twenty-five pieces of eight. The captain was in awe of the fine craftmanship.

Explaining to Leftee why could he not do such a fine thing! After being invited to a very fine meal and carefully rapping the sword in scabbard. They both said their thanks and returned to the ship. Because word had reached them that Samurai were about. The decision was to depart in the dead of night.

Beside scarring a few pirates away with their cannon. They passed the East-Indies blockade with no problem. Passing by night the same way south easterly, with a north easterly wind.

Caught in the quiet sea between the East-Indies and Afrique for three months, running out of food and water. They took to the two rowing boats, abandoning the ship. With what which seemed hundreds of miles and many days. One by one the pirates succumbed to the sea as their bodies failed them. To the last man the captain gave the axe to scuttle the boat. If he was not saved and rolled over into the sea.

One month and three days later the breeze rose and the ship under the banner of the Skull & Crossbones

sailed on its journey. Through foul and venture and one of the biggest storms known around the Afrique peninsula the unmanned Mary Celeste flying the Skull & Crossbones

was sighted seven miles of the port town of Plymouth. Where it was towed in and given a sombre welcome. As a ghost ship that no one knew where it came from.

This has been a indivisible story of a mirror image of anti-matter saw through mind over matter.

Dark matter expo

Dark matter is formed from the expansion of anti-matter.

Example : In the bar the stranger explains how someone he does not know called him by inexplicable names. Speaking words he could not ear mention himself. As he gets the drinks in saying he was the lowest of the low. That there was no other vermin to compare with. In the wine bar to a complete stranger the man goes up to say that he met a man. Who went on to say he heard you were useless in bed. That he would not be acceptable for a old granny. As he orders drinks explaining he was like screwing a match stick the ladies said. To top it off for a good time he did not know how to entertain such an exaggeration.

In the pub to the stranger he mention he met a person who said as he was getting the drinks in a useless good for nothing. That could only find is way around in the gutter.

That could not fight is way out of a wet paper bag and was thick as a brick.

In the lounge walking up and sitting down near to a stranger he made conversation. Mentioning somebody he met passing. He had said you were as corrupt as they come. Had no qualms about setting someone up, even though innocent. Ordering in some alcohol explaining that said was a back stabbing thief not to be trusted.

Entering the saloon standing at the bar mentioning to other at bar that meeting as leaving. Stranger had said that he meaning you looked like a useless stiff. That was a degenerate of his kind. Getting in the drinks to console the gentleman said that he was referred to as a wiener., fit to eat alive and spit out. Also unfit to walk the good earth.

At the pop-up drinks stand explaining to someone unknown. Did say how he was pointed out by someone whom had moved out of sight. How you had been said to be a sniffling runt. With the looks of a mutilated monstrosity. Offering to get a drink, further saying how you were good for nothing. That your life was not worth living. Prologue : After visiting the beautiful islands, having a good cold shower, having had a hearty breakfast. Did catch a taxi to airport for his luxury first class journey home.

As is shown did it not perform well. Did you see that throw.

Divisibility

Within a strange place and my being about to fall apart and become a new.

It comes to my mind that there is such a thing as transcendal meditation. So to transcend have you ever heard of conflication, that when inaugurated becomes conflictize. Meaning your mind is floating to devise.

I sit down on a beach and as I lay back on the golden sand. My body caves-in as I watch the sand become the placement. I am now surging through outer space. Looking for the point of magnitude. Where I can transcend into anti-matter sphere. As it seem like a age I am hurtling forth looking for the void sense.

Then a motion meaning passing within. There is no warning when it happens. It is just part of the destiny. From without within when it happens.

When within all I know does not exist. Just motion of many things, many beings., and mass change. All is a divisibility of this that and the other. From a it to a mighty climatic change. I was in awe and fascinated with everything I did. Like a never ending discovery. Somehow the blurred setting was always my main stay of my trek within until return strategy. It was a wonderous experience with the sighting of the sun on exit was cool.

Because my mind was coagulated as devise (not divulge). I knew that is would be disproportionate to total compound. As the reverse journey plummeted forward. When I opened my eyes I was back after controlling the sanding process on the beach where I started. Walking along the promenade I asked what date and year it was. From 1973 to 1974

I had lost and found a whole year.

Proving that when thought of transition to return. You are tossed because you are not divulged but devised. I cannot imagine if plans are not made to move forward with plan of senses. But it does prove a difference.

De – sensealize

Anti-matter is a divisibility of one self. The effect being a on mass accumulation of differentiating complexities. This is an aspect of where to find anti-matter. Is hidden by the many aspects of why an occurrence takes place. One aspect of this is Infectacide which deny the right to life. But are a form of existence themselves. Another being why people use a weapon to kill. But it is still that persons intention. To try and connect dark matter as something else is a complexity of the mind not understanding what they are in search off. A easy way to understand dark matter is that they are different forms of differences. A human that says something is dark matter just because they do not understand is in a quagmire of indifferences they do not understand. So it is cautionary to say it would be pulling at straws. Creating a false statement of belief. An example being is it a void or is it dark matter, is it a black hole or is it a liquid. If it disappears was it a form of. Statements of non-movement are not anti-matter. Which are like statements without proof cannot be classified as a positive statement of proof. Many sciences of today make the statement that dark matter is a unknown factor because there is no proof of. So what is a defamation of character. But because you cannot prove you try to influence.

Invisualize

I have just had a long conversation with a sociologist. That now thinks he is a expert in dark matter.

I went in for my appointment and explained. That I am losing my mind because my hard earnt money keeps disappearing.

He explained I had spent it. So I said yes I suppose so, but I have nothing in my home worth thousands.

He then said you must have invested it. I said I have no documentation worth 20-30 thousand.

So very well he said I must have spent it on a lavish holiday. But I said I have not been on a lavish expensive holiday.

Then he said you must have wasted your money on drinks and drugs. But I do not do drugs or drink.

Then the doctor said I know exactly what the matter is. As a matter of fact you never did have. You are in a dark place of denying the truth.

I said why doctor you have opened my eyes and mind to the truth. You know exactly where I am at. Thank you so much for everything. Where would I be without you. The matter of circumstances are completely clear.

Destructivity

An interesting fact if the planet earth is not going to be destroyed by the sun. With the expansion of humanity on earth, numbers evolving at a very fast rate.

With planet sphere having a white sun, where is it ? For namesake let's say it is behind the rainbow. So with climate change and the planet becoming in a more perilous state the more life goes on. So the heatwave has a bigger effect. Does that give anti-matter a better chance to expand. With a possibility of the rainbow shield collapse. Divulging the anti-matter verse. Would the rainbow form just become rays for anti-matter to expand. Another interesting fact is the discovery that black holes are more common than thought. Is one going to catch a sling shot for the earth. Or will they all divulge and tear it apart. If so is a black hole like a disintegrating format. Or is it a gate with a slip stream of magnitude to another spacial zone. If the format is the format then anti-matter would be looking at a free show of its compilation abilities. With the matter having no thought or mind-thought for expansion.

It is coming to a very interesting integration of a terror phenomenon. Of how to tear it apart and hoard the rewards.

Anti matter /
Mind over matter

- When someone intentionally does harm to another
- When someone is so saturated of energy they force themselves to go on
- When your mind closes down your motivation senses and you sleep
- When you are impeded on the road and you must brake suddenly
- When something is in your way and you must react quickly
- When you are sitting an exam and you must solve a problem
- When you are given a instruction and you must perform that act
- When you must remember you have a appointment
- When you are asked to do something but you do not want to because it is wrong
- When you are given alternatives and you must make the best choice
- When you know your life style is wrong so you must change it
- When you must change because of bad weather
- When you must concentrate to act on something better than before
- When you must choose what is best for you
- When you must choose between a choice of options
- What you think your girlfriend would think is best
- How far you would go before enough is enough
- Do you protect the many or the few

- Do you interfere in a confrontation that is not your business
- Is your families protection more important than your nation
- Do you fight in a foreign war
- Do you help the less privileged than yourself or do you make them sort themselves
- Is it right to help foreigners knowing you effect the lives of those around you
- Is it right to believe foreigners coming from war torn countries are refugees and not terrorists
- Should domestic terrorists be treated with kid gloves or treated like their international counterparts

Lapse, list

How long anti-matter would survive in a factual world is not clear. I only know that no human knows the answer. Searching the human mind none seems to have any knowledge of the personification possibilities.

The only fact that is clear is that neither of them are the same. But an interesting factor for make shift reason one does not know anything about the other. The proof of this is the dividing factor that one is incapable of making same as the other. Meaning that communication and level of English inadequate.

An interesting factor is that when one succeeds in forming as is another the only way for that to be divulged. Is for the factor of matter to deny the existence of anti-matter.

An interesting sense is to transcend into that matter and behold as anti-matter. There to becoming you need the knowledge to transcend, and protect that knowledge. By knowing what you're doing to not be dead on arrival because of stupidity. There becoming when succeeded into an amazing world of uncontrollable different views of amazement.

The point of knowing that when your energy levels are descending is when you sense that you want to remain as everything is because your energy level is flatlining. But you must understand that there world is not the real world. Then you will ascend to once where you started. If someone is in that place of entry you will ascend closest point to, giving them a shock of their lives. It is possible to remember, but it is better to create mind over matter. To be able to energize to a greater format and not be in danger of being washed out. Because you are in a sense of not being of no use. Sensing the creation and knowing where you are being is the important factor. Where everything is good natured as existence was. Then the further you can proceed in a unreal world. Do not under estimate the importance of being sombre in the belief of what you do. Or you just descend to what you are and the surroundings around you.

Obituary : Then cataclysmically unknown to you have disgraced the outer world and to the board stiff they think your loaded. Then because your way out there they will kindly let you know that they are no longer destitute and making millions.

Then solace is the nearest bar where you do not understand. The only thing you understand is the message in your head

' You had a good thing going '.

There blurred at the bottom of the glass which took a while to decipher

' What the heck , but you had '.

Transendanzycle

What is anti-matter if it is not anti-matter.

Where a person is a person but is not because it is that person. When connection is devised by a split moment of thought and transpired as a moment on a wave. Whereas finished with one kind, boy becomes another or boy becomes a girl or vice versa. Which is downloaded as mind over matter.

A very interesting procurement is the phenomena of the zombie cult. Where what is a human but not recognised as. Because over a time span becomes a cannibalistic being. With a craving to eat human flesh.

Science as delved deeply into how to reverse the process. But cannot find a connection between change and reverse for the symptoms. The human endeavour to survive as always been to gain sustenance from food.

So to manipulate the mind to one thought that is food would mean more. Their understanding a process of dark matter. Manipulate the mind de-generate the human evolution process. So it awakens Z meaning must have food like human, an very hungry. Because it has been disenfranchised from a normal human. How to survive is what the human is, a food supplement thought.

A interesting fact is when a human transcends and is suddenly awoken. With a whiteish sweaty face and hands. It makes claim to a horrific experience. Is that like when they are not them ? The horror is upon them ! So the horror of it all is not a usually seen factor. Like when for a split moment the zombie eats a horse or dog. There being an instinct moment of being a normal human. So the human format thought of not human prone any longer. So can it prone its human form to forget and become of another time-line. Where over an anthology of time it changes. To a sea creature with web hands and feet. Bright distinctive colouring. Long sharp teeth & claws. But would it forget that it came from the land and how long to evolve ? Who knows we are talking worldwide war, nuclear fallout, change of appearance, way they eat. There are different zombie formats. Some are fast, some are slow, some climb, some move quick eating just the brain. Some are water inclined.

To stop a zombie they shoot them in the head. But maybe they shoot the head because a zombie does not need a brain. It just lives of coagulated instinct.

So if a zombie is a baby is it furthering that instinct to develop into the super reactive zombie.

Is it only something that propagates. While the instigator does a runner. Or it is an accident in a laboratory ¿

P.S. Note : Have I just stumbled upon the anti-matter water verse in full bloom, where the zombie is the salt.

Matuistique

Before humanity talks war because it considers matter a good to go quantitative. With dark matter or anti-matter because of a space of consequences. Let us consider the armament and situation they shall be fighting for and against.

Where we consider the might of matter with nuclear weaponry. Weapons of exceptional speed and accuracy. Then there is inadequacy of so much poverty of a useless necessity.

Where greed over caring for others is non-existence. I think that is why matter ability thinks it is so great.

Then where we have anti-matter we have a spherical existence where matter cannot possibly exist. So two definitive weapons would be a malignant gun. Where when it comes in contact with matter. Would change it to a distorted noncommunicable non-motion image. Then there is a messatine gun which while distorting the vision of aggressor. It would also distort the mind. Till incomprehensible as a mind. Therefore a agonistic end.

Interesting factor is dark matter would need a power pack to enable its armament of attack.

But by vision it could create dark matter weaponry. But still use enemy annals of weaponry. Another fact as matter acquires through manipulation and strategy. Anti-matter would just use total annulation.

So no talking just defence. Then dark matter is a manipulation killer. Which has no qualms about reaching out to your weaknesses and eliminating as an obstruction. Or using one to interfere and be sorted out by a other. To gain further hold on territory. The necessity of its survival. So we have three constructive battle fronts. annihilation, manipulation and destruction.

So in a impossible scenario we have a lighted fuse burning at one end and a melting pot at the other. Then a time bomb of the have not on the side of matter because possible to communicate with them.

Dramatization

In the space-age search for anti-matter in outer space. It is very interesting to see that until their space ship reaches deep space there is no inclination of what it is looking for. They are reaching for what is then talked about as being dark matter. The wording of what is recognised as anti-matter does not get recognition until their space ship as been long into deep space (earth forgotten) and they are hunting other life forms. Where terror manipulates their weak petrification. There science is inclined to recognise anti-matter as a white sun shape or wave like motion hole.

With a thought process of passage is possible. It seems if it is confronted with a anti-matter particle. Its mental breakdown is of a non-existent format. That is tossing them into space. Or on a planet wreaking the laboratory of divisibility. The format of anti-matter taking out a whole planet is highly volatile. Where in a space ship it is like a mass of illusion. Which disappears its evolved. Before the seeing eyes. Shocking those that have caught sight of the phenomena. They then have a tendency to use what courage they have to say they shall go on. But have a tendency to make their research more to dark matter. This is not a statement against quality of a single expedition, it is a fact of many. Where each have divulged a further part of a unknown mass. A interesting fact is their further investigations always come up with the same result. That dark matter is particles of unknown origin and anti-matter is dangerous.

I do not know about the last part of the statement. But the fact that different science expeditions coming together. Then further their interest in anti-matter is a very volatile thought process. To recognise their identification of dark matter with weird goings on is very interesting. But to realize about anti matter and carry on. Words of wisdom be very careful. Also if they open their sub-conscious and probably do not like what they encounter. You will have problems far above your capabilities.

A good way to think is if you mess with dark matter is there any money in it, so are you onto a good thing. If you see something or find something that you do not understand. Make safe, jot down the particulars and seek advice. No matter how insignificant the particle in focus seems to be.

A good motto for the unknown is do not search for, let it come to you.

Both dark matter and mind over matter are very quizzical and interesting factions. Where a problem found a lot of times can be sorted. They both can be very cruel and heart breaking. So knowledge of the probabilities and a clear head is important in the procedural process. Many sciences talk of containment, so yes. But also do not forget it is a form of being. So take care of yourself.

Dramatization #2

So where are these facts. Lost in ledgers in outer space. Destroyed in a space craft incident. Destroyed by scientists that think humanity cannot handle such a finding.

The truth shall dawn, humanity has got so scared of the unknown it is tweaking out cheap guns link no tomorrow. Which has put it on a collision course with death. But be careful they do not create a fusion effect. Because of the recognise ability so a enemy creates a time of consequence. Then like the genocide war machine goes on a rampage. A good name would be accident incorporated.

Do not forget both of them do not care how many they kill in their life span.

This is an interesting factor that a human would recognise uncontrollable as a factual connection to anti matter.

P.S. Note : So look out, we pour the anti-matter finding a.k.a. particle compound into a gun let it settle. Then pull the trigger, and the findings are so gibberish because there is nothing there.

Exponent

As the rescue mission reaches the stricken space ship. Reportedly hit by a anti-matter burst.

The leader of the mission reads the report of the space ship on a scientific expedition, had left earth orbit over ten years ago. The crew then donned their space suits and three of them then drifted over to the marooned space ship. Then opened the air lock and seeing blotches of dark matter about. The leader then switch on his intercom and said. Tread wearily and avoid the particle damage because it is dark matter. Inside the gravity lock was off, so things were afloat. Also the instrument panels were off line. Hitting the reboot button the floaters came crashing down and the instrument panels began to light up. The air supply was again enabled.

Checking through the sealed door there seemed no movement from the dark matter. Trapped in the science laboratory and in the hallway where it had escaped. There were six crew members all accounted for and found dead. Three in the control centre, one in the hall and two in the science lab. After checking the personal quarters and storage all were seen as clear. Lead containers were quickly retrieved from storage and meticulously used to secure the dark matter. Then the containers were put in a refrigerator. Of the two scientists found dead in the lab. Their faces were all contorted in a look of terror. The others it was reckoned on minor particle explosions within their bodies. Settled on after a scan of their bodies. Caused by opening and closing of the sealed doors or through intercom connections. The six dead bodies were then placed in the supply room. Then documentation from flight plan, science lab and personal logs were collected. Over the next days the ship was given a thorough decontamination. With an extensive search for any contamination leaks. After extensive revision of the three logs. It was discovered that the crew had been trying to fuse dark matter particles together. As a way to signal an opening to anti-matter world. Which were the blotches of emptiness in appearance floating about the ship. Which must have exploded instead of contrasting, sucking out the air and closing down the ships instrument panels. Thus enabling the air supply and therefore unable to save any of the crew.

The containers in the fridge were then pulverized at a temperature of -2000°C.

Which left nothing but a yellow dust which was classified as the motion of evolvement between lead and anti-matter. An explosion charge of implosion propulsion was then set about the space ship. With a twenty-five minute timer. The final member then returned to the retrieval space ship. Then secured left the explosion area.

The mission was both tragic and successful. In that the finding of the mission in all research into anti-matter both within and part of must be processed with extreme caution.

Mind over matter #2

- When someone intentionally does harm to another
- When someone is so saturated of energy they force themselves to go on
- When your mind closes down your motivation senses and you sleep
- When you are impeded on the road and you must brake suddenly
- When something is in your way and you must react quickly
- When you are sitting an exam and you must solve a problem
- When you are given an instruction and you must perform that act
- When you must remember you have an appointment
- When you are asked to do something but you do not want to because it is wrong
- When you are given alternatives and you must make the best choice
- When you know your life style is wrong so you must change it
- When you must change because of bad weather
- When you must concentrate to act on something better than before
- When you must choose what is best for you
- When you must choose between a choice of options
- What you think your girlfriend would think is best
- How far you would go before enough is enough
- Do you protect the many or the few
- Do you interfere in a confrontation that is not your business
- Is your families protection more important than your nation

- Do you fight in a foreign war
- Do you help the less privileged than yourself or do you make them sort themselves
- Is it right to help foreigners knowing you effect the lives of those around you
- Is it right to believe foreigners coming from war torn countries are refugees and not terrorists
- Should domestic terrorists be treated with kid gloves or treated like their international counterparts

Dark matter

- Things that are not of this world
- Things that are hard to believe in
- Things that people say are going to happen in the future but you do not believe them
- When something is true but no one else believes you
- A catastrophic event of unbelievable aptitude
- When you are told someone you love as passed away
- When something you believe in goes drastically wrong
- A war within your country
- When people tell you lies to manipulate the truth
- When something is acted on against your belief
- Foreigners that gain entrance to your country and perform wrongful acts
- Act of aggression towards other person or persons
- Use of inappropriate actions to make gain against another
- Baring arms without just cause
- When you are fooled or forced to believe false words or actions
- Those that lie to gain from false statements
- Those that would make false representation
- Those that would dyfile or dephimate your beliefs
- When a curse is put upon you
- When an action receives a negative reaction
- When something is not as it seem

Anti matter

- Something that is not of solid form
- Something that has no life form
- Something that delves in one identity
- Something that believes in sharing on mass
- Something that has a consciousness
- Something that cleans house periodically
- Something that recognises one as all
- Something that believes in chosen future of its own choosing
- Where something is nothing else is
- A moment that has another moment to look forward to
- Something with a clear sight to the future
- A treasure trove of dishonesty and fact
- Something that can be given but not taken away
- A ever changing atmospheric upheaval
- Something that forms what it is
- The mirror image of annihilation of all others

This mean war

As mind over matter unleashes its fomenting.

Unwinding courage is unleashed. No mind before can stand up to its ever changing carnage. As the first sign of hope is lost in words. Now dawn is breaking like the ground cracking. Thundering forth nothing can stop it on its endeavour. To wipe out any that stand before it, like a nightmare grows all around it.

Coming from whither and therefore it moves forward. All are no match as its mind is drained. As it goes home to rest and recuperate. Thus the braking of the dawn and a new day once more into the breach. Knowing it is not over until it is over. Where peace is coming from whom is to know as trivia is soon forgotten.

Is this dark matter, ask it as we shall meet as the red sun rises. In our fight to the death, two shall go in one shall return. To the victor shall go the spoils. As the lightning struck in the clear bright sunlight the hate was instant. With one stance said we fight and die here. The other screaming like the raging suns kill um all. There the blood bath took hold with the unleashing of bullets to their sort destiny. With arrows seeking out there aim from position of attack.

Seething with anger other forms of attack were unleashed from the darkness. Rifles on one side spears on the other. Carnage was rising reaching for the sky. There in a feat of rage because of a matter of fact. Out of the shadows rode hate in full bloom. Where with knives drawn the true honour of live by the gun die by the gun was tethered in death. Where then a strange calmness rained as if it did not happen, until the next time.

An anti-matter think what is this monstrosity of idiocy I am surrounded by. How is one to get any peace of mind. Does anyone have an inkling of care. Look at the place is like a bomb exploded. So who is going to clear it up, to you do not know, o yae yours truly who else. This in the brake of twilight, as the enemy scream victory is ours. Like a vacuum of remembrance a torrent never been seen before crosses before them. Leaving just an inkling of what was there and the sense of what now.

As dark matter would look and think I must do my duty an seek victory. Peace must be maintained at all cost. With the echo of the spirit, if you do not get it right then what is your share ?

Anti-matter / Wild mind

As Isaac Newton sat under the apple tree under the moon lite sun. Then when the apple fell upon his head. In human intelligence it is said that scientist Isaac Newton created a paper proving the existence of gravity.

Furthering his investigation he was to extend his knowledge to the imaginations of space exploration.

What I am getting at is an infringement of fact. With the unknown realisation that when Isaac stood up he did extend his mind into fifty-million particle compounds. That did open up the realms of space. He was kept alive by how slow and meticulous each part of space exploration must be taken.

You can dyne the said fact but do not forget that Isaac Newton did leave his mind in proven space. So what is found out must be proven facts. So we have right of vision of what is and the facts you believe. So what is the belief that got you there.

If I say nothing do you believe me ? If I say findings do you believe me ? If I say mechanics do you believe me ? If I say experimentation do you believe me ?

So if I say particle compound do you believe me ? Whereas humans say everything has DNA !

Do not fret if you think it is gibberish an does not make sense. Just think facts are facts.

P.S. Note : What an amazing person to have just glimpsed such wonder of mind over matter.

Verse

A terrifying assortation of spacial upheaval. When you have a clash of Aliens where matter verse is just a common fact. Where it destroys itself and if not is destroyed by something it does not understand. Aliens use other embodiments to create new life. Sometimes killing the host. Then there are the Triffids where matter is only something to digest and compound the fact that it once was. Triffids lure in unsuspecting prey. Then there is anti-matter where dark matter is constructed if obstructed. Creating an ongoing destruction on the attacking force. Dark matter which displaces matter and creates devastating destruction. Then there are germs which create abominable suffering for matter compounds they infect. They wear the mask of a bandit looking as if they are the mirror image of anti-matter. Living under the synopsis of 'get me some o that'. Then there are germs that no matter the matter distort the body or the mind. In what can be agonising and prolonged circumstances.

As others fall aliens through lack of appropriation. Triffids fall through lack of nutrients. Germs cease to contaminate because of inappropriate atmosphere.

Anti-matter is a totally different thing. Whatever the opposition is, it will fight to the death. In the enemies existence. In its being the particle is now of no worth. It disperses to another form of its surroundings.

Whatever the facts these formulations in full flow are devastating and leave total destruction.

Anti-matter / Matter smash

While traveling in my Orbital, time machine I decided I wanted to try making a transparent transformer. Which would change the appearance of the orbital. After working on the digitizing cannisters and dyonic crystal I placed it on the right side of the Solaric. Then I connected it to give it a read out purpose. I then decided where and how I was going to test it. Then set the time to new world beginning 1638.

There upon arrival I decided to rest the orbital of the west coast of Briton. Upon doing so I clicked the switch and before I knew it a four mast frigate the Skull crystal was in my focus.

I then did a skimmy around ensuring all was of the era of time. Well satisfied I got in a row boat and beached upon the shore. There I tangled the tavern and dock getting me a crew.

Travelling the corridor of the Mediterranean sea we dealed and delt. Upon the journey seeing the emptiness was when I decided to search out anti matter. Returning to Briton, then with an offer to the crew of the ship, information, plus charters for trade in the new world. We set sail for America where my quest a new was to begin. Where travelling, discovering and experiencing anti-matter I completed my folly.

When sighted for the next beginning it was as I expected. The time continuum was not settled for a breaker. Ripping through me like I could feel myself being ripped apart bit by bit. It was as if I were feeling every moment until I was nothing. It in the end was as if my whole being was gone. All I felt left of me was a speck of existence.

Then there as if I existed for eternity I floated whom know where. Until I was at the Orbital. In search of a unbelievable catastrophic existence. Where caught in limbo I am just waiting for a whole new beginning from once I began.

Anti-matter / Tributize

As one is anti-matter, then it cannot evolve because it is. But when the chain is broken and dark matter form is triggered.

As anti-matter evolves in motion as a sense of one. Dark matter rises with the equivalent of negative sense of being.

Where now it dark matter as a sense of one itself. It shall grow in negativity where chaos reign. As something is it shall seek what is not. Then just be more of what it is thriving on the plus energy from evolving dark matter. The problem science is trying to eradicate is the uncontrollable energy consumption which happens with dark matter. What is wiping out the wanton science is the mental capacity of dark matter to become more skilled at draining negativity from matter. Only the mass of anti-matter is different to dark matter. Where anti matter is one dark matter will destroy to become more of one. As matter is an energy consumer it does not look good if dark matter as a want to gain more of itself.

It is very interesting now to divulge the what is a nuclear force. If anti-matter is one then dark matter is zero. With the evidence of matter saying it is dark matter. Then dark matter equal minus zero. $1 + 0 - 0 + ¥ = 1¥$ which is a 99% chance that dark matter is fusion Mind over matter Is a very dangerous and destructive motion to matter. Where something is but when is isn't it is not. It can also if the pursuance is pushed be of no more. Matter is a very easy form to be made no more. In science search for divulgence !

$1+0-0+¥=1¥ = 0-1-0=-1+0=-1$

Where there is a negative supply of matter there is now anti-matter.

F.T. Note : If you have 0 and add a negative to it why do you not get 0.

Protraction

Back in time people used to ask what happens to you when you die. Used to query what is on the other side. In sleep mode people have awoken claiming to have had a wonderful dream. Others have awoken sweaty and disoriented saying they had a terrible nightmare. In the 1700,s dark matter was first mentioned in the analyse of science as a unknow phenomenon. Not knowing if it existed or not. When then came the discovery of gravity and the mention of the saying anti-matter. During the dark ages and medieval era phenomena was recognised as strange magic. Now science is slowly saying it is dark matter.

With space technology caught in a void science is attempting to grasp at the element of dark matter. Preferring it to anti matter seeing it as a safer alternative. There are mass dangers in this search seen in the wake of a nuclear explosion. But science has turned around and said that there are many untold discoveries to be found from dark matter such as a vast energy source. Whatever humanities persistence the magnitude of danger evolves greater with the more energy perception created from the dark matter source. There are many questions to be asked such as it dissolves in a number quadrant how does it stop. If it enters a energy source does the after effect cause a explosion or die effect. When you have a enclosed effect what is it search process a.k.a. radioactive material.

Does the radioactive material act as a transmission arial for its quest. So if it finds fusion does its arial transmission act as the area it finds to destroy to create more energy.

A interesting observation is the Philadelphia incident in America, the Chernobyl accident in Russia the Fukushima catastrophe in Japan.

Have they been irradicated or is there a underlying factor. The search for control of dark matter has to be...

core - dark matter - negative = stability

Now for the million dollar question if you synthesis what you have. Will you live to tell the tail. Or will the anti-matter fusion divulge nothingness. A interesting phenomena is once anti matter is discovered. How do you find the mass of it. Dose the mass retract or increase on its use. Or is it embryonic where it does both. At what point would it create photosynthesis and fusion to anti-matter take place. It in its deep universal project, do you really think synthetic DNA would make sense. You and your unknowing will your findings be calculable. A interesting thought when you consider its atmospheric effect is totally different to the earth atmosphere.

Astronomically

I have heard a person refer to a void as a gate way to anti-matter. Where entering you become emersed on the outskirts of another world. A void is not a window to the realm of anti-matter. It is a barrier to protect life forms from the anomalies of space. Anti-matter is a sub-tonic wave of exponentials that transverse each other. To create a lasting existence. Its only connection to a world of solids is where cities in space exist by expanding and retracting. With the connection of the spacial transpondency of the space of anti-matter.

The future of anti-matter looks very promising with humanity laid to waste because of its inadequacy. Then there are the contagion blockers that used to ensure the human continuance, but they are no more. There is only anti-matter that can give it change or it dies. A interesting thought is what will be the controllable factor. The highly prone anti matter sequence or the attitude of humanity.
The divisions of knowledge between differences is only a drop in the ocean. Compared to their true quality of being. Beside the facts being fake, they are idiot to the fact. So being wise to the fact of anti-matter can be a toxic a.k.a. stupidity if you think DNA makes sense. The only reality of anti-matter I have found as intelligent is Tesla having to have the need of assistance in proving mind over matter. Facts do not create a reality. Acting upon facts create what is your surroundings.

F.T. Note : What we are going to learn about !

If my intelligence is correct. The aspects of creation are Matter, Mind over matter, Dark matter, Anti matter.

Matter (I'm it) Mind over matter (Think sod)

Dark matter (I don't know that might be dangerous) Anti-matter (You sure about that).

So "I'm-it" big deal if you don't "think sod" we are done for. Yes correct but "I don't know that might be dangerous". Okay then "you sure about that" brainiac.

Now your purpose for living until you quit is to prove your purpose. Or undeniably anti-matter has won.

Understandable

As the mind evolves the passage way to anti-matter the Aon in the mind starts opening. Showing you the incredulous destiny that awaits. But then comes useless sense such as scared or do not understand. So then the Aon in the mind closes down. This state of mind keeps repeating. Until you reach the realisation pinnacle you can close down the matter interference. It can keep repeating to the point off unimaginable pain probably death. But it would be the same eon experience because it is on a different cause to matter. There is no other way to avoid the Aon experience divide from matter. But once meaning when you finally have eon flow in the mind your connection with anti-matter being you slowly begin to realise. First the Aon begins to grow and your sense of being is there for the taking. When the eon process does end once there you enter a void. Then your oneself becomes a cell structure. Which goes through a meticulous change of matter to a anti-matter drive force. Where matter existence does not exist. Where on a eon drive you shed your existence. Then in an empty moment the ion drive to anti-matter is set on motion. There to reach somewhere a vast anti-matter assemblance.

Any particle compound is a dark matter effect. That fuses mutilation to ensure the anti-matter evolvement at end of journey. The finish of the journey is like a fusing last white light as a nuclear fusion disappears. There to the unseeing mind's eye is the fact that matter has nothing to do with it. There in the last moments of the past you descend into another being of you.

Bubblistication

As one is asked what is the matter

As a matter of fact, of a matter of time and space.

It does not matter what I do not know, where what I know matters as much as it does.

As in a question of ethics I push the matter because it does not matter.

Where when it is on my mind I question myself over and over because it becomes the facts of the matter, until it does matter or not.

The fulfilment of the matter is what is important. Because it is important to insuring the situation is correct.

If it matters search your mind until you improve your quest unto the finish.

It is better to understand what the matter is or you could get very mixed up.

So let us take in and dwell upon the matter then sort it. Before nothing matters and it is out of control.

Now sit down and tell me all about it. The matter in question is it serious or a trivial matter that is bothering you. Whatever the matter is you can get through it.

The scientist says it is getting dark outside.

The impatient man replies, what does that matter. Then for the next two hours the scientist goes on about dark matter. Then the impatient man says, stop ! Not one word you have spoken as made sense, so give it a rest. Then the scientist replies I have a BA, PH,D and a master's degree, so what I say matters.

The impatient man then says. I do not care what you think, so take that for anti-matter.

The scientist replies their there what matter.

So what is the matter with you.

More ancient than time itself. More devouring than humanity can understand.

Without anti-matter you have dark matter. Meaning end of the known universe.

Mind over matter is the beginning of the end.

With mind over matter I kill you.

With dark matter I hate and want to destroy you as you die.

With anti-matter you want what you cannot have so I annihilate you.

Vetification

In the sphere of anti-matter there is an array of weapons of mass destruction.

There is the Viral velociter a weapon of terrifying capabilities. If enabled it can dormant the arteries in the brain to thinking it has only one thought process. Leading to nothing causing a collapse then death of the body system.

There is the pulse-ring a weapon when fired emanates a pulse which shatters cell structure into its smallest form. Creating dust and rubble of solid structures.

There is a Shieldic that acts like a shield that when tempered sends out a demonic wave signal. That can turn a nuclear missile back in the direction in which it came.

Another formidable weapon is the Lavaric multi which when fired sends burning pulses through cell structures. Creating a matter lava appearance. Which can ascend to phenomenal heights in temperature. Their kind of weaponry is created when an outside force tries to diminish a anti-matter protocol. The distance of the wave only diminishes when the threat has been terminated. This potential is a rarity in the universe because of its existence as a celestial body. The potential of hyper active weapons from the anti-matter sphere far out succeeds its anti-matter embodiment. Which clearly shows its potential to protect itself. The existence of anti-matter an potential of virus venom velocity to extend its existence clearly shows an impasse is inevitable. Which means mass destruction of the obstruction because existence to carry on is not possible.

The effect of matter contagions on each other is a continuous area of destruction. Dis-similar facts of this are not an anti-matter deprivation but a form of one being.

Bomblistic

A interesting thought is what would happen if anti-matter factions. Meaning mind of matter, dark matter and anti-matter were to collide in there instrumental formats. Such as mind of matter verses dark matter or anti-matter verses mind over matter.

There is a parallax that if not deciphered has meaning of looking at disaster. If you have mind to does that mean the complexity of dark matter has to be a trivial. Because you are looking on in a terrifying unbelief.

If anti-matter fuses with dark matter is the dark matter a lesser one or is it just the same different.

If mind over matter fuses against anti-matter. Where it has lost its mind, as no self-respect for itself, feels sorry for itself, tired. What becomes of it when shown where to go.

Then there is the sequel of many against one. Where some against one thinks it is equal. How what to do but put it in its place, which is nowhere.

You take my eyes, I take your face off. You are in my way clear as death. The only parable you have now is as you perish the poison that caused it. You walleur and pay through the space time continuum. Then they care, you deserve.

There are many parallels in the Anti Matter verse but then there is only one ending. That is death to them all because they are not wanted. The orb is motivating, now dwindling and there is only one force at work 'what is not'. Now in the divisions of your human being you are transpiring to the you say you came from. Because it is stinging you to death from once you came. It is not ethics, it is no other. It is you and only you fit for it. Grasping with all you have for what.

Stickwas

As the eye of the anti-matter eyed beyond the gigantic foundations. On the mind shall they attack in wave formation or shall the best advancement gain most. It was clear to see they had no intention of getting stabbed in the back. As mind over matter came at the foundation from the right flack. The matter flak from the left. With dark matter taking the centre flack.

The battle was fierce with matter forge being held and weakened by the shieldic response.

On the left flank mind of matter did not fare much better. But with their technical advancement in various formats. They were holding their formation. The battle was like a spectacle of flame. With both opposing forces wanting death and annihilation of the other.

The dark matter force was like a forge to be reckoned with. Forging forward in one stance then another. With anti-matter holding fast. Matching fire distortion with each dark matter move.

With non-stop battle with raging torrents of fire energy from both sides. Again an again the diversity charged at the foundation. Then again and again anti-matter raged in with the attitude of next please. The sense was clear all round. You are wiped out with the forge to accentuate the tact. The failure was clear when anti-matter got in. It is together they were dust. After a year of battle the diversities started to think they could regroup. Anti-matter shattered their appearance until non-existing. After not being able to regroup it was clear a biological- nuclear warhead was coming. But the encounter raged on in bits here and there. The strange thing was nobody gave a darn about hate. It was just left on free fall. Then in the solemn quietness of yours is mine. Nuclear-biological warheads were exploded here there and everywhere. As if it did not matter.

Looking around seeing all the devastation and lost body parts. It is not that I am forgetting the injured. It is just that in a screen of dehydration there is no pain. It is just a encounter of whatever.

In the forefront of thought process it is over. The anti-matter Z frantic lurches forward with one intention. That is explaining it is not over until it is over. With a terrifying non-stop strategical onslaught. Leaving nothing alive but the sight of victory. With dummy nuts explaining its life away.

The headlines now things have settled down, dido graphing on the north. Discusses the situation of its circumstances.

The south mentions in stoned I do not know what you're on about. With the inclination of look at that.

The clearest fact is warriors lost in time is they take no prisoners.

Mind on matter

Mind on matter is like a jigsaw with what come naturally you have to think about it. Because of all the particles. If you think about it is like navigating a worm hole. Where you are trying to get a solution and you just cannot figure which particle goes where. But you are persistent because you know there is a outcome. Giving you satisfaction when you succeed in your quest. But mild irritation when you realise a persistent problem has a simple fix. A fascinating thought is if you brush aside the particle compound. Where in your mind would you go ? To do this it would be wise to give a thought. Example no equals yes giving a clear mind warp of mind on matter. Mind of matter is a simple understanding. Such as what to do with yourself. With thought there is the action. Then there is the ominous stance. Such as jealousy, conceited, sorrow. So mind of matter is thought imitation, transparency. If you create a complex you have to follow the irritation, then there is a dissolving aroura. Strange fact persistence make perfect. Mind if matter is a strange phenomenon. When you are in sleep mode and you are factual reading. When getting close to the answer the thought process disperses, without a final outcome. But do not worry if you calm the loss and transcend the mode you should get facts to fact answer.

Mind to matter is the sense to be careful with nightmares. You understand deep sleep. Especially if you have dropped out of a void. Then it is all so clear. Then there are fantasies, dreamscapes.

So we have mind to matter, mind if matter, mind of matter, mind on matter common factor matter base. Which drives the thought process. If the mind creates a thought process is it a matter compound or just a transcendental process !

Fractuos

Anti matter : A sepheric body that has no solid form

Anti-matter : A divisible quantity of the structure

anti matter : A divisible particle of the structure

Dark matter : A lone particle

Mind over matter : Where the brain creates to form a purpose

Mind of matter : Where the brain is divulged in sleep mode

Mind on matter : Where a development is created in the brain with a solution

Mind in matter : Where the brain creates a imagination

Matter : A solid creation

State of matter : How something survives in its existence

Dry matter : Something that rations existence in everyday living

Wet matter : When a foreign body attempts to survive on another. But creates a negative effect

Invisible matter : When something is described but the object is given no mention

Raw Matter :

I do not recognise the place from when I was last here.

Saturated Matter :

When a particle compound can go through no further change

All matter is unstable or can be made unstable.

Wet matter

In the beginning there was anti matter. Which thrived in the existence it was. With a enjoying capability to survive. Then to move into wonderous sights of being. This chain of events does not seem to have lasted the test of time. Because the existence of anti-matter is a very false belief in planet earth understanding. It is fantastic to think of its existence when planet earth seem as a failsafe.

When it comes to dark matter which is a particle of anti-matter. It is easy to see the mass of existence anti-matter survives in.

With no element of proof it is hard to understand the volcanic eruption. Under the sea taking in all of the pacific ocean in less than two hours. So I am speculating it was a wet matter experience. I think only the islands stopped its claim on the pacific. A very dangerous game making claim to what is a incapable achievement of survival. Which now I am under the conclusion that the pacific tsunami was a wet matter abstract. Because as is dark matter it was no mistook creation.

It is quiet the vision the sighting of manticulation. When you realise any mistake and like so you are a speck as the unfortunate.

Dark matter is a very unstable quality which makes me suspect it ignited Mount St Helen in Oregon, U.S.A. Because after the explosion the volcano structure was very different.

A interesting phenomena is the forest fires that have ravaged North America. Where because of global warming, insensitivity towards the environment. Invisible matter has become prominent. With reflections of what is then is not. Where heat from the sun is put through a reflexion change. Which creates fire instead of warmth.

These causes are glass reflexions, heat build-up and burning heat from touch such as metals.

Then there is Dry matter a very inhospitable atmosphere. Where it is near impossible to grow anything. With no air to breath existence is improbable.

Whatever the matter it is a chain of events that has created the sense of the forming of the anti-matter sphere.

Dreamscope

Welcome to the anti-matter space entity. I am sitting in a library reading about the different matter verses that exist.

Namely Anti matter, anti-matter, anti-matter, dark matter, Mind over matter, mind on matter, mind in matter, mind of matter, matter, state of matter, dry matter, wet matter, invisible matter.

Each particle of complexity seems to have a different purpose and the only connection is nothingness. Where something is, it has to be nothing for something else want to exist.

It is as if when something formed then what was left of the anti-matter was used as a energy source to give purpose to that being. I am wondering through like drop by drop it passes. I sense that the process must not be broken or completion shall not be possible. Leaving damage limitation to finish or end. Because it is a cycle there is no going back.

It was a case of what shall be shall be.

All the different particles are now slowly coming together. Now beginning to swirl around moving faster and faster. Then the thought of emptiness like sleep. I then awaken I must have been sleeping. I look and see I am sitting at a table. With a stack of books on it. Looking I see dark matter, mind on matter realising they are all books of the matter verse. I then pick them up to put them somewhere. Thinking where would I be if I journeyed through all these forms. Then I think nowhere because I have just been. I go outside the surroundings all look grey and different. Everyone is moving around with a purpose that they cannot see (like a invisible matter verse). Where when completed is just a shadow in the mind. Now I am drifting and falling deeper and deeper. Where everything around me is irrelevant. Until I reach an impasse and I have passed to another state of matter.

Cazaclystik

The process is evolving as if one grinding in and around. Now it is going round as if stopping. With the speed getting faster and faster. But then speeding up the other way. But just before it does it is like a massive intake then outtake of energy.

The lights are bright getting brighter. To the point of like a blistering meltdown. Then the blistering pace of the meltdown changes as if getting darker and darker. Then the sense of cold getting so very cold freezing cold like a implosion.

Then an emptiness takes over the sense draining the being to nothingness. Now looking like a foreseeing void. It is as watching imagining as part by part the being is ripped into pieces part by part. First the outing, then the sum of the parts, then the main compounds. Ripped in pieces repeated into bits. Then repeated again into specks. Until all that is left is something of nothing.

Now everything is just like a void of quiet stillness. Where the only existence shall be a beginning to end. Just the sense of aroura of what has been exists, which grows as a energy force. With energy proceeding and gaining in intensity. Now you look upon a non-existing entity a.k.a. anti matter particle. Which is and is not it just exists. It moves around in a form that the eyes adjust to. But cannot say if it is in slow motion of different motion. Then when there is a flash change in the anti-matter. Like in a moment what was a particle is not. But is how the energy recedes or succeeds. To the sense where it is a particle of one as is.

This process is called anphibilation where what you see is what you get or is it.

Where the particle hits hyper drive is where you have de-composition. So what was once was anti-matter.

anti matter,
Anti matter, anti-matter.

As the Anti matter mind becomes a is not and then becomes an anti-matter particle. Then it sense what is as anti-matter. In the different spheres of education like a rigmarole it navigate. Traversing its being finding existence is not. Then to be as a traveller it divulges until empty space is its domain.

Sitting around the table drinking the tavern dry. It say are any of you ready to set sail to find the unknown. So as quiet settles about hark ; a voice " are you drunk or summit".

Grim reaper : say look at me do I look gone. You get me what I want or you get no shilling.

Himiawouthar ; he will do it cause need is greater than the woe.

As he return with and passes the drinks round Jaqulle comments. So what we going to talk about now.

P.S. Note : I look into my world and think how wonderous you are. Now any moment I shall be overwhelmed. Then both of us shall be no more.

F.T. Note : Now no worry Green-back all is clear keep on it.

Okay guys you all here, then I shall get the drinks in. if its intelligence is wrong I mean right this is how we are going to do it. Well this is it or is it not, does this does that. It such a sure thing that imagine, just press a button and that is it. No more this that or the other just that is it. However created that how smart was it. Continents discovered just over two hundred year back and they got existence way back when. Understand what I am saying, yes, their existence was just virtually yesterday way back when. So they cannot be another being ! We are human and what you see is what you get. Are you listening you do not look so good. But you claim to know everything. So it is a good thing as the smoke clears there is a new thing or is that just different. The claim on existence is all different. I'm it shall not win it is just I'm it. So payback reign supreme.

Galvanetics

Incredulous credulous commodity credible commodity.

As I scan the area , as I move towards the shade of the area ,as I fade into the shadow of the area , as I scared the kid / as I throw the knife within a scream of the thieves eyes.

All that is known can be terrifying to know.

A paradox on the right to life, which side shall you evolve on from a state of matter.

A interesting factor of a persistence of being is the ability that gave the availability of matter transfer from the cart to car to plane.

Now science is in search of particle transfer meaning to send a solid from one point to another in a moment. This is sort through dry matter transfer. Where a particle is displaced into a atomized solventzie at one point and replaced as a particle proportionate as was at another pre-ordained position. Within the expedience of the movement a interest to the fact is the time distance propulsion. Where within it is articulated as a fold through or bionized as a elasticated shoot through.

Far into the distance of science discovery is the coming of the discovery of the invisible matter space suit. This discovery will come about with the intellect of mind of matter. Where one takes the mind formulation of its creation and in that moment becomes that space suit in that atmosphere for that amount of time. Where sleep deprivation, tiredness, inability to proceed, inadequacy of capability would give warning signs to get off or pay the consequences. The fact you are a foreign being in that sphere is just a prelude to your actions.

Historicismos

Where spheres collide and a historical moment does appear to occur. The point of origin is where what are you on about. Because origin as gone sepheritical. Because big bang as no numerical value. Before all the questionable ability is lost a numerical value of zero is equal to the answer. So if there are three part anti-matter equal to one. Then there are no equal division to one that is. So the divisions of the equal are all different. Meaning no one are the same because they are of different. They are all different as one is. Where the divisional of one, then you have the creation of development.

So where you have autonomous you have creation of automatic development. So as if everything is broken or disappeared. Does anyone have any idea what it was.

So : 1 + O = -1 or is that 1 + 0 = 0 because it is dealing with negative placement. The paradox can be found in the unequivocal compound of question, solution, answer. De-generation of the void can have a disastrous effect if you are in search of answers. So the formula for anti-matter is the sum of all the parts are was equal to.

Now as we you or whatever get temperamental everything becomes of a temperamental unequivocal understanding.

Where we now have bodacious partialent brake through of quantum physics, mechanical physics, nurobiontics

A good example is imagine you have a gigantic well equipped laboratory. Then you have partial formulae. Your intelligence equals success. So do not forget to take home your discovery. All interesting anomaly are still in the journals. So easy to understand yet the facts do not exist, they be just theory. Another interesting anomaly is the factuality it does not have. Then no one can have.

Inversination

Anti-matter............ Matter

Nothing.................. Something

Decimation .... Desecration

Some .... Plenty

Few .... Lot

Extinction .... Destruction

Noise..................... Sound

Decisive .... War

Accumulate............ Annihilate

Transparency .... Solid

One........................ Group

Quietness............... Echo

Boom .... To late

Is, that is .... Is, that off

Part....................... Bit

Infinity .... Time

Mysticism .... Encyclopaedia

Slaughter .... Battle

Concoction .... Sun

Never..................... Always

Before.................... Present

Contagious............. Oxygen

Living .... Knowledge

Different .... News

Prognosis .... Death

Movement............. Flight

Energy.................... Food

Demonize............... Disenfranchised

Sense .... Watch

Energetic................ Enjoy

Prevail................... Change

Divulge.................. Signal

Togetherness .... Classification

Plight..................... Being

Other .... Preference

Bestow................... Plunder

How precise this senses is unknow !

Come on professor time to go, no I shall remain here, no it best you come with us, I said I am staying here,. Now this shooter is loaded and knocked. Now get out and leave you do not have much time.

Anti-matter / Obsorptional

When trying to write a summary about anti-matter you find yourself writing a dialogue about a particle of anti-matter.

When the mind is natured on anti-matter it is not because it is the substance of matter.

When travelling in the sphere of anti-matter you are not because it is not there, you just think it is.

Anti-matter is a vast instantiated knowledge of nothingness.

The connection between the brain and anti-matter is where the mind leads matter can be proven. Where anti-matter lead the brain cannot substantiate.

The purpose of anti-matter is to create disbelief in fact and beyond.

Anti-matter is a vast shallow of emptiness because the brain think so.

I am looking into a orb, what I see is I shall make a space rocket of anti-matter because I know everything off.

I am looking into a orb, what I see is I shall make a space rocket of anti-matter particle. Because I need a instrument panel.

There is no connection of where the anti-matter particles are connected. Because of multiple phazability holdings. Example mind over matter where start is to end and finish is central.

When the brain is pierced with different anatomical instruments the wave length intensity are different. When anti-matter is pierced with different anatomical instruments it meaning that is met by different explosive intensity.

First rule of anti-matter mind over matter.

A diagnostic of anti-matter is the accumulation of the compounds to the connection to the final connection for to the creativity.

When activated a simulated particle must be able to fuse with the anti-matter.

All parts of anti-matter are a sequence of a whole of anti-matter.

Anti-matter is not a negative thought of matter. It is a negative thought of what matter cannot prove as fact.

On my left I have a particle of anti-matter and on my right I have a particle of anti-matter. But they are both different. Which is more ? Can be seen in how you perceive it.

Anti matter first contact safety, anti-matter first thought war, anti-matter first sense extinction.

Anti-matter at first awakening, a load of nothingness.

Where anti-matter formulates is from beginning to end to formulate. Where difference is to change.

A problematic conception of anti-matter is that it does not exist.

Valaristic

The anti-matter puddle swoons and sways to be inspired to be of a moment.

If a distinction is not of another then to transpire on to that would not be possible. A simple aspect would be to explain it could breathe in but not breath out.

But where one is a part of in some form. Then transfix is given as a part compromise. But the same thing from a beginning would be a sense of. Meaning unlike all DNA are different which is where the discovery of the universe came before things. Then the divulgence of others aka diseases, anti-matter. The sense of anti-matter creation of another works in a sense of a millionth of a second. The only partial difference is the which part of the other anti-matter does it create. Does it care ! so reckon with it cleans house, destroys foreign bodies on contact. Always ensuring something different to divulge onto. So securing anti-matter always moves on. Creating a new which can control the time paradox to its ultimate possibility. With holding different to more differentiated. Without causing a gibberish aspect to a wrong format of survival.

Endocromical

What is anti-matter, how does it exist, what can it be used for. I hope reading my journal it is possible to have come to a better understanding of what it is concerning.

While writing my logs I came to realise good opportunities for the future. With the endeavour of anti-matter particles. With its purity and high energy capacity. It has the ability to improve and make better. Example the earth space program. Which looks to be caught in a time loop. With a lot of talk to do things, but without the knowledge of how to do it.

If planet earth keeps on wasting its resources with repeat endeavours it will make itself so incapable it shall be unable to survive. The planet is now on its last journey of hope. With the mouth of the commercially rich. Spinning a yarn which is just making more people poor. The human attitude that anti-matter is to create enough food for one to feed ten is just quickening the extinction of humanity.

The closer planet earth succeeds towards the sun. The less it is possible to replenish oneself from the riches of the planet.

Scientists say within one-hundred years humanity will be unable to support itself on the planet. Meaning within two-hundred-fifty years the seasons shall stop existing. So then photosynthesis becomes pulmarick pollination a semi-solid contagious inadequacy. Meaning the destruction of the planet. If humanity does not reverse the polarity toward the sun. Then soon the quickening will thrust it into a inevitable ending.

It shall not be possible for the north-south poles magnitude to stop the eclipse of the sun splitting the earth in parts. Where the central part magnitude will pull the part planet towards the sun. With the

lava vortex creating a de-fusion polarity of division. With the part eclipse emphasizing the remaining.
All this happening as the planet goes dark meaning all communication link between outside bodies are severed.

Corisation

A strange quizzical belief of the unknown is to cause a creation of unknown. A mysticism of the unknown is the mystical non-understand of the unknown. Which can create a transfixed obsession of indulging in that unknown. A paradox between the sane and the insane is the sane call themselves psychologists to prevent the growth of insanity in themselves. So is the unknown between sanity and insanity where the psychologist would theorize in which way the unknown leans towards sanity or insanity.

A strange perplexing from this unaugment is the finding that if it is not sanity or insanity, then it is a unknown entity. Deliverance to this empty place would have to be on a flatline protocol. Because mindful thinking generates thought. Then the thought is of what is hidden in a unknown entity. Is it a nightmare or a fantasy place. If you are to believe the human aspect then the body would die because of a unknown growth. If we are to understand the findings of how to develop and succeed. Then the host is just a void of that person what is. As another is not of where you are coming from. To understand a transpire is a massive undertaking. Which would take a time lapse of work, study, experimentation and with cost.

This is a good theorization of thought on how the detrimental aspect of anti-matter was first developed in what it possibly could be.

Intersecting the doctrine of anti-matter it creates one aroura. That being to transpire must be periodically endorsed by one saturated knowledge. The thought, the knowledge, the aspect is how I have and have drifted into anti-matter. Through its thought, through its being like all been a part off.

Where anti-matter divulges then many a part of divulge give a mass expanse of being when possible to imagine.

'Where one was is' are magical words between the what is and what was.

So divulged as bad is just another form of saying it is no more. Where matter rots and decays it is referred to as no more. Which is not scientific, so a quick intake of anti-matter is a good cover instead of probablized. Then before crinkles, specks, then dust. Which is not anti-matter because it is not.

Matterlistic

Antimatter compounds as a phenomena !

Anti Matter : Where the sea flows all that can be saw is far as it want you to see.

Anti matter : As the fish swim in the great sea, what kind of fish is that.

Anti-matter : Where there is quantity, a part is a part of the mass.

Dark matter : When you know something is there because you can see it. But your intellect can take you no further.

Mind over matter : If you do not understand something then you never shall until you do.

Mind of matter : I have the plan, I have the materials, all I must do is put together to have.

Mind on matter : Where everything was a load of parts. Now you do not want until you close your eyes and rest.

Mind in matter : Where everything becomes a blur from sweat and turmoil just before the dawn.

Matter : The facts are clear but how to figure the facts.

State of matter : If it is still there as you say then you have to prove it.

Dark matter : I cannot understand it when at the start it looked like there was enough.

Wet matter : We have held up here and now look we are worse off than before.

Invisible matter : Rain what rain your eyes must be deceiving you.

Raw matter : I do not recognise the place from when I was last here.

Readings

Getting closer to the finish of what has been nothing but a fantastic journey through the sphere of anti-matter. A strange phenomena has been the dissolution of wording when trying to explain in the words of human reality.

A interesting fact has been the right of vision of a log as not been set forth until the log has been completed. It has been absorbing, interesting and intriguing through-out. The ability to divulge beyond the unknown has been enthralling. A fact of finding about the read-out has been the uncontrollability of prevention when instigation is of equal. The understanding of discovery from a point of knowledge to a journey end as been a vast undertaking. Which I in my own quest I leave this planet shall show a passage through out space. A interesting fact is the factual findings of which could be the different configurations of the sense of anti-matter. Where within one to all is anti-matter read out formation finish. Which creates the end of the beginning unto where to begin. Before their beginning what do they absorb before their beginning. It is interesting to notice that a greed and thieving contaminants is a near if not potent death wish. Which is why probably it is easy to understand the finish of planet earth. With space bludgeoning the planet with every mutation it makes. Where which part is putting it together or is putting it in parts. The diverse ability of survival on planet earth looks to be diminishing faster and quicker with each procession in time. Which creates the breaking point of the parts is what part before the number of parts is beyond saving.

Warning Sign : The easiest way to jump of a cliff is to read the signs and know. Where there be triffids, aliens, zombies. Knowing there is no humanity there. Where there is none there is different. What happened to humanity I do not know.
Matter

Sightings

An interesting observants in my journey quest through anti-matter has been indivisibility by the human mind. Because of its vastness of not being a part of human endeavour to succeed into the future. Where humans have made claim that disease on planet earth such as germs have been around since the beginning of time. Anti-matter has not been thought of until space exploration was thought of. A first mistake in human time exploitation has been to consider disease has been around since the beginning of time. Whereas man ascended from the forest did it not find trees and flowers. So a strange expectation would be the unequivocal belief of humans did this and did that on the planet.

But starting with the belief that planet earth was a germical dioxide that created a earthling beginning. Where that was devised as a untruth with a creation of the sun.

Which diminished the planets responsibility for self-reliance. So looking to the future if any part of this creation cycle did collapse because of incalculable adequacy. Then negative edecacy would be devastating toward survival of humanity.

So if humanity is creating a formula for human survival and a sector of humanity is creating inadequate living conditions. Is humanity not creating thought positive and negative theism. Meaning a dark matter mis-construction.

Where walking around on what is left of planet earth. The air is a musky grey appearance, with clouds that spurt out deadly lightning bolts and acidic rain. Where flowers are non-existing, only weeds are visible on the ground. Which is just a quagmire of dust and melted land. Where one of remaining humanity, waring round rimmed glasses to protect her eyes. Searches the ramshackle city for food or survival things. Only finding a broken window that looks drip dried. A refrigerator that only looks half there with the rest melted away. Any wood still around with a touch turns to sawdust. Then returning to her encampment thinking so that is all the dust laying and floating around.

So does that mean all that this mean is a fire ball from the earth core to in a instance decimate the earth to nothing, from once it came.

Longevity

If a human walks on hot coals it is said to have been possible through mind over matter.

If a human sleeps on a bed of nails it is thought to have been possible with mind on matter.

If a human cannot understand something after scientific experimentation they refer to it as anti-matter. If a human irritates, provoking then releases a nuclear blast it is referred to as mind in matter. When a nuclear blast occurs creating a terrifying scenario. This is thought of as dark matter.

If a human makes, uses, discovers, changes, divides. It is seen as mind of matter.

The matter of a difference is created by cell division. When understanding does not mean you understand what now has become from the matter change.

When this is referred to the matter of the circumstances. How can that be when it is no more.

A good way to divulge a steady proof of change is to refer to the complexity as in a breakdown of algebraic deduction to the Constance.

Where there is a state of matter after an explosion. Is the after effect the particle remnants of what was or now what is. As to say once was, now once is.

As is anti-matter and it becomes part of what is that part is not anti-matter it is anti-matter.

Where the sea is the sea which is forever vaporising in the hot atmosphere. It can only be recognised as invisible matter because it is still there.

When you have a container explode because the surrounding atmosphere is wrong. You have created a wet matter fusion.

When a bomb is dropped and it does not ignite. It then transverses into a state of corrosion. Then when it explodes you have a dry matter experience.

When you have saturated matter, which has been all it can be. It becomes nothing of cellular structure.

With the once dead sea, became a salt bed, then dried non-existence.

A time of raw matter. As the earth is drained of its minerals for other purposes it changes its structure to a raw matter reaction.

So everything becomes matter a meaning of knowing which everyone understand.

Massamistic

Question : Do you know the life expectancy of a human.

Answer : The time of life before death.

Valuation : You forgot the magic words,

'forever more'.

In the far distance there is death, in the far far distance death becomes you.

The Invision of existence in anti-matter is a slow non-realisation of a divulgence.

As the sun rays evolve giving life on planet earth. It only receded when the saturation of matter creating further matter reached its limit. With the sun process it creates hidden life with photosynthesis in plants.

As a butterfly is formed from first eggs and then hatched inside Lavi. Still a life forming and then it became a caterpillar. Which then transforms into a butterfly. Which can circumnavigate in the atmosphere of the planet. The creation of the butterfly is called metamorphosis. Which is a changing form of matter.

It is not the sight of what it is I am trying to show. It is the something that is not then that gives for a form of creation.

This creates a thought with the mass of the sun and the many of the different butterflies. Where you have a large amount of anti-matter in any form. You have a great amount of something that has no weight, except in micro manipulation.

Where you have noise you can have an echo. It is said to be created from bouncing of a solid object. But to have a recourse of that noise there would have to be a viability of how and what with the change took place. Which creates an image of sub-sonic change to allow for the reverse of the matter. Interesting factor is dry matter for the change, but is still of the kind noise to echo. Things change in many, many different ways. Where matter is fused as is moved. Examples being where someone runs they do not create a solid footprint or if two colours are mixed the reaction creates another colour. Where is an amazing insight into how is different where it was there. Again creation of a new beginning through dry matter.

Through all the differences there is the Invision of invisible matter. A interesting fact is as the cell structure brakes down or creates an acidic compound then that development is forgotten in existence. Not recognised as a matter of fact.

Where the performance of an aeroplane cracking the sound barrier. The split moment of quietness before the sound of the big bang. You have cell structure of the atmosphere taken to its limit. But where does the structure of the cell structure that goes to the noise intensity go. Does it return in form to where it were. Or as was it in a state of saturated matter.

So with giving saying anti-matter gives nothing. Is it not proof that anti-matter give but there is nothing to receive.

Dictatorial

As I delve into the anti-matter star burst colours are created and movement does begin to exist. The particle compounds are formed in many a rearranging segments of form. As it bursts out into the expanse where existence is welcomed. The existence point of anti-matter does become as is at its saturation point. From where it were particle wafe to change it did progress. Now it begin a folding space expanse to once where it started. Where one is not only difference being, where matter does not exist. So then particle of compound of anti-matter does transform through its time and space. Where once is in so many different ways creates all that is anti-matter. Where change does not exist except in sense of anti-matter to the existence of saturated matter. Then where is not is only created through expanse from what it was once from when it did begin to change.

This is an ecological myth that the big bang was not in a beginning. But in a steady commencement of creation. Where now is anti-matter as it divulges the best of its belief for creation of further more. Off that which is different, where now anti-matter does not exist.

Now at the eye of anti-matter it is interesting to see a fantastic realisation of everything that is not of this earth, planet earth. Created in the non-belief of anti-matter but what it perceives of its worst problems.

Explanatory

In my experience of my journey through anti-matter I have discovered that it is a tunnel vision experience of belief. With the answer to further understanding not shown until the particle of anti-matter has been transpired. Where all of its negativity is proven neutral. Then the division is complete and the connection of another protocol transpires.

There is explained how a begin goes to a finish, before another moment of existence.

All my facts are coming in word because in the dark matter sphere nothing is singularity. With a possible many or few different sequences for the probability from once it is. The moment of disillusionment in the dark matter sphere are when you do not understand, lose track of the particle journey, or have a illusion that it is not possible to further progress. You can find your thought beginning to enter a flatline phase if you get anxious. But it perspires when getting close to end it is explained.

The journey is of one long journey through different segments of anti-matter. From a journey beginning through-out the sphere of anti-matter to a journey in where anti-matter is not a consequence of happening. The face of anti-matter is all different, with the same outcome. That is a new beginning with different ficids of the anti-matter particle breakdown.

To succeed is a clear emptiness with thought. With a build-up of thought only found within a catalyst of anti-matter particle transfer in sequence to survive. The clear equinox of disbelief and the danger it could endorse is protected by the different one perceives to the other.

Distinctually

A figment of the mind is a figment of the imagination. A imagination is a thought of the mind that does not exist. A creation of imagination is a thought process that when manipulated through an image creates a matter of being. Which is a transparency when looking in a mirror of dry matter. So when you look in a mirror what you do not see is the creation in through the mirror to what is the reflexion of what you observe.

It is not what you look for when you look and cannot see. It is what you find when it was not what you were looking for. This is the parallax of the wondering mind. Which is a window to the matter verse. Meaning when you look now your mind has found foresight into finding in motion and sight what is matter which is all around you.

Now beyond this because of the thought process of what is the unknown thought of what is beyond existence as disappeared anti-matter.

As I look now I wonder as the particle moves on. O well if that is it, I guess that is all there was. So be it as it transpires through the adjoining features of anti-matter one by one. To the bitter end, so now to the bitter ending.

Until it is no longer a part of. Where passing through where to next is all it has to offer. Until sense is made of the nothing it shall try to offer.

So relax I understand what you are trying. So what you are saying is what it is saying is not true. Because you're saying it and what it said is just say so. Then there is your saying that does not make sense, but it does because it is not true.

Now coming to the end of what it said and is said. Once talked about to the death is easy to see that definitively correct is what was mentioned properly.

So after the observer is board tired and states that nothing said has made sense. The only way to come to a correct answer is to see after the conversation which falls asleep first. Then the one left awake is correct because is explaining it.

P.S. Note : Make that a ton of tea & coffee, Hundred-fifty reels of tape, a phone line, all known genres of dictionaries.
This is going to be a long day.

Now let see where were we, o yes if chaos sleeps in another spectrum of space what are you talking about.
Don't forget about thirty packs of cookies and some cake.

Labyrinth

A carnivorous brake down of wording into words. Meaning there are many facets from start to finish in the exploitation, study and understanding of anti-matter.

The beginning of the journey are wording to open the mind to what dwells in its meaning.

Then the technique to where the entrance to its being exists and how to find the gateway.

The best part is the gaining in confidence in the search the longer it goes. Always being as best in control of your trekking is of utmost important for health purposes. Once reaching the window it is important to abide by the rules of engagement to enter within.

Once within it is a closing and opening the mind to just a sense of what is the surrounding around you. Then begin a commencement of sensual change as the journey of multiple difference in anti-matter begin and end to start again.

Where there is dark matter there is a difference it being that it is a single entity of anti-matter. Where with anti-matter there is a sense of change to another of what is.

With dark matter the changing connection is a negative impact. Usually in the resemblance of chaos, a.k.a. devastating contact.

When with mind over matter it is a state of action to a re-action. Which then does not extend in existence any further.

The assemblance of anti-matter is a quest where within lies different momentums of transversely. There is a understanding fact of why dark matter is so volatile.

Anti-matter there shows an existence of atom variations of a singular thought of anti-matter.

Where fusion of its various containment visibilities devises and transverses to various particles of differences in what it is.

The fact that anti-matter can reach a saturation point and still hyper extend its existence is very clear indication of a mass energy source. Anti-matter is clearly a divided source of existence that transverses in one of many.

An amazing finding is that once the deteriorating transcended fact that the anti-matter being is no more. Is that what was once is now just is in the passing spherical of its destiny from the start of the journey.

Uniqivicalize

Through-out myself taught inquisition on anti-matter I have researched three main factors. Those being Infection, Future, Unknown. Throughout my writings of fiction I have come up with facts. Which I have sensed have proven my writings to be thoughts in statement.

With all the facts and information I have found no connection with them to Chaos, Supernatural, Paranormal. Which are other facts of unsure and unknown statements of belief. A interesting fact of the paranormal, chaos and supernatural is they are the last bastions of the internal frontier of human discovery.

Where you have a situation in a confined area where normal actions do not exist.

Until fiction is finished in fact any attempt to coerce statements as true would be a course of danger and should only be tried shrouded in safety.

Where what usually transpires does not go with the surrounding actions. Creating a moment and scene that is recognised as chaos.

When something happens beyond your mind understanding. What does happen you cannot understand how or why it occurred. This is considered a supernatural occurrence.

When your mind registers a happening that does not register in actual happening in reality. But is caught on sensory instruments. This is known as paranormal activity.

KC - S2 = PN1

If the facts are formulated in one does that mean the answers will always be formulated in the three of the parts equals the one or minus the parts equal the one. Or is there a connection between the parts.

Whatever the answer to the phenomena, the answer shall only be found after the parts are put in particles of fact to create an end. This is a solution of the formulation of the parts.

Because the formulae is trice over each part must be broken down to create a answer before it is possible to formulate a connection. The way to do this is to take each part and break it down into as many understandings as possible. Then create a meaning and try to connect into one of all the differences.

When the particles have been saturated you try to add the parts. If they add together the answer should be correct. The interesting question is does anti-matter exist within the compatibles. How would you find out if you do not know about all the qualities or the dividing accusations. A interesting fact is all the qualities. Where would the human race come into the equation.

In chaos you have mental qualities but they are all on a different wave length. Communication is only made in a negative moment. Solids that are supposed to work in Cognito do not. Any connection is a destabilising momentum. All that is supposed to work together works but does not as it is supposed to. The degree of correctness is a very low percentage.

With supernatural configurations there are a occurrence that are not supposed to exist on the planet. They are strong, scary, and thought as dangerous. They are considered to have amazing abilities beyond human comprehension. The abilities are totally different to a human. With paranormal they are thought of as people who have passed on. Trying to communicate with the living. They are considered to be able to reach the living through wave lengths. Such as phones, cameras, sound. They are not recognised as a living thing. Any evidence is usually said to be a equipment failure.

Chaos, Supernatural, Paranormal are all mutual collaborations. Chaos with incorrect thought, Supernatural with imagination, Paranormal that are thought of as inequality.

P.S. Note : These factual compounds do not seem to have any proof of connection with anti-matter. Fusion that develops within might develop without, But then it is not, a passing thought moves on to where and develops it until they are no more and then moves on.

F.T. Note : The solar exploration by anti-matter began. Where is it now but out there somewhere.

Parsycline

By the deformation of anti-matter I am referring to what would become of anti-matter in a after format.

To figure to find I have took everything to a particle state of being. Where you have anti-matter you now have chaos. Where all thoughts and living are not what they were recognised as. Now you have a neuron network that is not connecting in a stable anti-matter atmosphere. So tensions begin to rise and the sense of right and wrong become a fact. Meaning the understanding of harm and pain. In a state of nurtured being it in time would forget and lose recognition of its past.

This is a form of change in where paranormal activities would have a chance to process to form. Where the mind knowing one thing. It would have the intent to want to know the opposite. Where a form is how can it be shown as a different. Where say the mind seen before. But another reads that thought. With so many different moments of mental telepathy. There is created an image of modes of the supernatural. Where atmosphere is but with different purpose. Which different formats of strange existence being the common.

When something is recognised as different and only seen as evil when the eradication of its all is given a reason why it does not exist. This would come about through boredom. Saw as forgotten of or forgotten because it was only recognised as the normal in the past. The ending of it seeming like a distortion of the mind. Unable to think in it once whole of being.

In the different facets of anti-matter dissolvement creates a facet of many wonderous images of magic and sorcery. When the talk of it used to be many. Thus being lost in the annuals of time. To be only remembered as legend. Where without the correct atmosphere or potions there would be no returning to the past.

With the advancement of their capabilities they have inadvertently made one existence to another a unbelievable fact. Where only mythical belief of a existence before dinosaurs and humanity ever existed.

Now it is a world where knowing not what they are doing humanity is creating nuclear power claiming it is going to this that and the other with anti-matter. Where its mentality is just to say the word. Where its ability to dissolve and destroy could be stopped. (Breaking news you would have a heart attack at the sight of such a happening). Because the awakening of anti-matter would have its own purpose. Such as the solution to paranormal activity, supernatural and evil.

At the expense of wickedness or part of the human vocabulary.

I think it would be quiet a wake-up call for humanity to see what space is made of. Thus realising how trivial its abilities on the planet are compared to what is out there. Human mentality thinking everything is possible at the wink of an eye, is slowly closing that eye as a obstinate failure.

Whatever it thinking anti-matter is way ahead of planet earth thought process.

It is like seeing humanity as just burnt to stay alive by getting warm round a fire.

As the human walks away from the fire then returns. Have the other gone away to dissolve into the abyss which is chaos or been wise not to return because fire as stopped burning.

The facts are not clear about the particles of beings of anti-matter. But what is clear is the one vision of intent of everlasting.

Parsycline #2

For an explosion of a catastrophic nature in the anti-matter realm. You would need a negative evolvement of a matter compound an a form of anti-matter. Such as dark matter or invisible matter. Anti-matter is a divisible quantity within its own sphere. So when it devices within it selves it creates a positive endeavour.

Meaning they are compatible. But when you have a solid you create a pressure point, where a negative and positive come together.

So the more the solid matter tries to obtain from the anti-matter the greater the pressure shall grow and be needed for the solid to be of a useful significance. It is as you have atoms flowing to create what the solid is for purpose. The more pressure is applied by the anti-matter to create a negative flow. Then when you have to many ions of negativity. The solid eons begin to break down because they cannot counter balance the influx of negative flow. Thus creating the change of the reaction of anti-matter with the solid. Which unturn results to a unstable condition. Which can be deemed catastrophic. Because you have the anti-matter charge fluctuating through the solid and expanding in energy force.

Anti-matter is a form of pye but has no insignia. Because it is not known where it is coming from. Just that it creates then recreates which gives it the unknown capabilities of energy. Just the different readings of what it once was. The possibility to recognise the potential of anti-matter are disguised in the type of anti-matter used, the potential for and the atmosphere it is used in.

A good fact to recognise is the looming potential of a dark matter growth. What would the energy level be if it got out of control then went on a free fall. Is the energy burning out or rising ! I think this is the creating of a catastrophe.

When you try to create an atom from fussing wet matter and saturated matter let's say. Would you have the potential to control the energy output. Looking at all the different facids for creation. I also see they are throught with danger. I know all experimentation is dangerous. But to those around you that know not what you do, is that not different ! All calculations of reaction should be read first. Then only carried out in growth particle by part. Under a safety and purpose protocol.

Do not under estimate anti-matter uncontrollability is a substantial part of its existence. Then to stop it you need energy that would cloak it in its guise. Where the important part is it is a usable ability. A horrific conception is if an anti-matter particle is broken down outside the sphere. Would it make way to a form of anti-matter outside of containment and cause a positive or negative reaction. a.k.a. a ticking bomb scenario. Because of a creation of a unexpected overload.

Parsycline #3

A intentional examination of experimentation is what would happen if you fused together particles of anti-matter.

Would it be a creation of another form of anti-matter. Then there is the potential of what would be created.

This form of experimentation would be very dangerous. Because if you mangle it in an atmosphere where the solid is unable to contain, then a dangerous situation is created. From either the anti-matter particles or what has been formed.

Before attempting such a experiment you must contain. Because different particles would have different energy potential.

Learning and knowing about each different particle is an important fact. Because the coming together of differences could lead to different scenarios. Such as a new anti-matter format, a changing format of new anti-matter, or a crossover format. Here noticeably is the potential of a possible creation of a invisible format of anti-matter. Then there is the fact of would it change the potential of the original experimental particles. As everything is not as it seem here is experimentation that should not be taken at face value. After the findings are diagnosed are there lingering particles lying dormant In the matter controlled experiment area.

A good way to ensure the safety protocol is to have the neurone network contained within the solid of the experiment area. Not a connection to an outside source.

Here is getting into the thought of when it is performed and if the experiment is successful. What are the potential energy readings, time of particle solvent, end of use moment.

It is a scary thought process, which is very stadlising to write about. Scientists performing experiment would be in a dangerous and unknown environment.

An interesting phenomena is are all anti-matter particles compatible outside the Anti Matter sphere.

My (Covid-19) thesis / contaminant

There are many different disease types now being found on planet earth. They are put into categories of bacterium, germicides, viruses. They have a varying capability from highly toxic to mild symptoms. The deadliest before coronavirus / covid-19 was considered to be Smallpox which came to be known as Bubonic plague. Two new viruses being mentioned in the 21st century are Ebola virus discovered in Africa and Monkeypox discovered in India.

All disease infections seem to have been found in a localized area. Then have spread rapidly, taking in the whole world. All seem to have a wide damaging effect on the planet.

With a cure only found after the disease as caused wide afflicting damage.

There is a major concern arising at present with the newly found infections of Monkeypox, Ebola virus and Covid-19. That is there has been no permanent vaccine against the infections been found. Infection findings and spread as basically originated from one of three factions. They are diseases created in laboratories. Made by scientists by mistake or intentionally. There are those diseases created by unsanitised living conditions. Such as Ghetto, Shanty town, Slums. The third is micro-biotics being released by global warming. Where virus, germ, or bacteria are being awakened from melting ice caps or destruction of natural habitats.

Mass disease is being spread by water pollution of the sea by oil spills and sewage discharge. Another is drug usage with sheard and dirty needles.

Major problems are A Systematic carriers that spread but do not get infected by the disease. Systematic carriers get infected and spread the disease. Both contagious to the uninfected. Where we have vaccines and the cure is enabled. The infection is stopped but then forgotten. Leaving unpreparedness from any further outbreak. Then there is the fact that vaccines take time to create and distribute amongst the populous. A greater danger is if the body builds a resistance against the vaccine use.

The important factors are protection, vaccination, prevent. Education is important but so is stopping the culture of greed over security.

Defaced

In the near distance future when sycosis as reached the tardiness of cleanliness for all. Where there is any inclination of any kind of disease outbreaks fines and threats of imprisonment are rampant.

People both foreign and domestic are being terrorised at airports for any despicable reason of domestication in their own nation or where they arrive from.

Pharmaceutical companies are at the forefront of it all. Making massive profits for unproven drugs. Which are causing dangerous and deadly outcomes including death. Facts are clear that stringent security measures are being breached. For what many refer to as profiteering. When scientists can sell unproven drugs. Say the drug works then a few month later the immune system has no effect against the disease, example being covid-19. Another example is a disease trying to get out of Africa. Under the same pretext is Ebola virus.

When an American nurse caught the infection cured then returned to U.S. Then died of the virus in America.

Pharmacies a.k.a. scientists know very well that over prescribed drugs will make the victim unresponsive to the medication.

These people that live in a digital age with what is not theirs to behold are corrupt through and through.

Knowing nothing at least the many that died in the past from mass infection. Lived and died keeping their respect. Giving all powerful vaccines for the next generation.

Where the spin is what was saved meaning contained and created A symptomatic infection on mass. Meaning the disease shall trek another track of contamination.

A glimpse into the future is biological contaminate. Where amalgamation of a D.N.A. formulate will allow a false identity to enter across borders. Which can be DE structuralized once destiny has been reached. Because the D.N.A. is a dissolvent. It will become a transparent decadency. To use as a entrance way to a purpose of survival in a foreign nation.

Deployment

Getting into where the future lies within a medical aspect is a very interesting and terrifying diagnostic.

That is your vision through all the sickness has an inspirational vision that there is hope through all the infections ingrates. With all hope depending on the accessibility of medical facilities providing quality products.

A negative factor of that happening is the medical fraternity and its science not following the strict protocol for devising protection against deadly contagions. Where the mere thought of the terror politicians and public outlets demand a quick fix. Before all precautions are proven and endorsed.

Where the protocol of under one flag and one people is disregarded for a deteriorating immune system. To almost non-existent and expecting to survive where the quality of life does not exist. But is slowly shredded to a non-existence of once was. Where a meaningful life will deteriorate to become a simple ending because of no disease protection, from what would take of life.

There are two factions forming with the deteriorating of existence. One in which disease pandemics are inevitable in the future. Being more contagious than the previous. With no protection from the immune system, which was substantiated approximately in 2020. The thought is very ominous.

Two is the war factor that because of population expansion and food harvest unable to keep up nations are going to require land for productivity.

The hope of many is going to be strained to the limit where trust shall slowly wane. Meaning war for preservation of humanity is a powerful antidote for survival. Against those that would deter the survival of the few to spin the fake greed of the many. The clear aspect of the many that have destroyed their own way of living. So the words of death shall be given what they are creating destruction, elimination, war. Then the survival instinct development to overcome the failed immune system of the past. Which was caused by false recognition of a necessary security. Where want of another does not make sense.

Destopia

I have added my thesis of covid-19 because it is as close to anti-matter as humanity has got so far or you could say it was a warning from outer space.

My thesis of the covid-19 pandemic has been coming forth since the outbreak in December 2019. The pandemic has caused chaos with economies throughout the world. It has destroyed families showing no mercy in its endeavour. The medical fraternity has been in nowhere land trying to understand the virus. As it is when it tries to explain anti-matter.

Like a mirror image it as evolved with change like anti-matter. It has the same sense of mass destruction of anything which gets in its way. Like anti-matter it as only stemmed its flow after total fulfilment. As with only partial outbreaks of the virus as with dark matter with the thought of what is to come... Without a irradicating vaccine the spread of the virus cannot be stemmed. It will manipulate grow and possibly cause again a very serious epidemic.

The problem with covid-19 and its self-manipulation will that be the same with dark matter manipulation. With the cell division of the virus antigens what will be the outcome of anti-matter growth.

Interesting observation is :

Covid-19 biological warhead wiped out the planet earth

Covid-19 biological bullets wiped out neighbourhoods.

Covid-19 biological landmines spread across counties like wild fire.

Covid-19 bombs penetrated defences and initiated the virus spread.

Covid-19 grenades are particle compounds which when exploded are like particle shrapnel.

So does that mean a grenade is a neurone configuration of covid-19 particles in different formats. So these minor surges the planet is now having might be probes for the annihilating of a covid-19 biological grenade attack.

That is to say the collective decisive particle division to cause the natural distortion of humanity. Will this be a first of the coagulin attack or inductive of its presivist.

Doomwatch

In the space-age search for anti-matter in outer space. It is very interesting to see that until their space ship reaches deep space there is no inclination of what it is looking for. They are reaching for what is then talked about as being dark matter. The wording of what is recognised as anti-matter does not get recognition until their space ship has been long into deep space (earth forgotten) and they are hunting other life forms. Where terror manipulates their weak petrification. There science is inclined to recognise anti-matter as a white sun shape or wave like motion hole.

With a thought process of passage is possible. It seems if it is confronted with an anti-matter particle. Its mental breakdown is of a non-existent format. That is tossing them into space. Or on a planet wreaking the laboratory of divisibility. The format of anti-matter taking out a whole planet is highly volatile. Where in a space ship it is like a mass of illusion. Which disappears its evolved. Before the seeing eyes. Shocking those that have caught sight of the phenomena. They then have a tendency to use what courage they have to say they shall go on. But have a tendency to make their research more to dark matter. This is not a statement against quality of a single expedition, it is a fact of many. Where each have divulged a further part of a unknown mass. An interesting fact is their further investigations always come up with the same result. That dark matter is particles of unknown origin and anti-matter is dangerous.

I do not know about the last part of the statement. But the fact that different science expeditions coming together. Then further their interest in anti-matter is a very volatile thought process. To recognise their identification of dark matter with weird goings on is very interesting. But to realize about anti matter and carry on. Words of wisdom be very careful. Also if they open their sub-conscious and probably do not like what they encounter. You will have problems far above your capabilities.

A good way to think is if you mess with dark matter is there any money in it, so are you onto a good thing. If you see something or find something that you do not understand. Make safe, jot down the particulars and seek advice. No matter how insignificant the particle in focus seems to be.

A good motto for the unknown is do not search for, let it come to you.

Both dark matter and mind over matter are very quizzical and interesting factions. Where a problem found a lot of times can be sorted. They both can be very cruel and heart breaking. So knowledge of the probabilities and a clear head is important in the procedural process. Many sciences talk of containment, so yes. But also do not forget it is a form of being. So take care of yourself.

Immuneablous

The effectiveness of the immune system with so many variants is becoming ineffective in holding back the virus surge. People are hoarding all kinds of drugs. But most are having no effect in holding back the virus surge. There are two factions forming. Those that believe in the booster vaccine program and those that believe in the anti-bodies gained after being infected. Both factions are commenting that with anti-bodies when it again infects the subject would just get sick but rarely die. Ignoring the fact that the disease infection keeps getting more smart against the immune system and anti-bodies.

We must devise and gain all the virus variants and anti-inject so the virus is nullified.

The gemauglon, group factor of different infections are a different factor. But we must start somewhere and degrade an nullify its, their ability to kill humanity. There are too many negative factors been put out in the world. We must find and control the protein. Then prevent negative factors devastating or mis-guiding the truth. From what is absolutely necessary to find and procure.

At the moment covid-19 is fathoming around and as not passed bad as of yet. But the flare-ups are an anxious moment. Another thing to be watched is since China claim 98% of populous was infected with loss of life put at thousands a day. Nothing of the virus has come out of China.

To be clear no new variants is a good thing and hope is surges can quickly be bought under control. Right now the world is on tender hooks and India is running scared because of the latest wave. With problematic infections being found in children.

Lullactive

What is the lull before the storm !

As the world is on tender hooks, saying covid-19 is like a influenza infection. Reports are just of sporadic outbreaks.

A nightmare scenario unwinding is the virus winding down for a explosive infection spread. What with many countries burying their dead instead of following safety protocol and burning them.

As the worldwide spread of the virus began to form another process of developing its antigens through photosynthesis in plants. Then a new effect through plants and animals. If the disease is beginning to change through mass effect. With the use of weather change it could create a catastrophic effect.

With animalistic deterioration effect, or a sensation of to die like plants. With a devastating effect of control of survival on the planet. Death as the normal for life loss, it will become deterioration of the number of population of the planet.

Where there is word said that there are many things undiscovered on the planet. A permanent protective vaccine has to be found. Where I am becoming sensed to protection and survival. What is unknown is deteriorating into a dark matter phenomena.

The savagery and takeover of the change needs to be sustained with a purpose of resolve. With the killing of the virus with ever stronger covid-19 deterrents change of approach must be looked on as good. A potent spread of the virus on the immune system would be devastating. A slow steady procurement must be established and perfected outside the mainstream. So science can be thorough and serve its purpose.

Medical statement

Russia : Good day I am your surgeon, if you die tonight you shall not live. If you awaken tomorrow then your still alive.

America : I do not understand we have the best doctors and hospitals in the world. Everything is out of control.

China : Three years after rest of the world recedes from pandemic. We are declaring a national emergency. Ninety-eight percent the population is infected with the virus and our drugs are no good. We shall not allow foreign vaccines into the country.

Australia : We had everything under control, but now everything is falling apart.

Great Britain : We are being eaten alive, so I know nothing.

Europe : The virus is sweeping across the country. You are our neighbour, so you are next.

Africa : Everybody is infected with the virus. Everybody lives in the countryside so we cannot get a vaccine to them.

India : At $1.24c we can get a vaccine to everybody in just over a year. At $2.50c we can get a vaccine to everybody in just over two months. That is why vials of out dated vaccine have been found dumped around the country.

Latin America : If we live you live, if we die you die, who cares about your vaccines.

Statement : Pharmaceutical companies have made billions of dollars from so called vaccine that fail in months and affect the immune system.

Mind boggling

Three things have been happening since the virus outbreak. One : climate change has been rampant. Two : cost of living has been mind bogglingly high. Three : The virus has mutated and felled any barrier used to stem its flow.

The cost of vaccines to every country on the planet has been very high. What I have been trying to say is what has been done has not been of any adequate push forward. So if the three factors are over lapped. Would it be possible to make a diaphragm diagram of where and how a permanent protective cure can be procured. A good base for this fact would be the multi-millions it has cost to create a failure of a vaccine so far.

Using a three time factor where is the over lapping. Given the longitude, latitude and directional finder. Meaning necessity for a proper cure. Giving an ability to know how and what dosage shall be required for the vaccine. This would procure a nice profit as a finder's fee.

I have been looking for a cure all my life. I have no idea if there is a possible hope.

Where facts are stated you could use the alphabet or numerical calculous I think. I am not pussy footing around when I say no one deserves to live with the damage caused by weak vaccines. Stated to be good because inadequacy by pharmaceuticals make sense to governments that do not understand. It is heart breaking to realise that biological science can be so protective and used in such a harmful and destructive way.

Organisatie

There are many organisations around the world that have stood the test of time against the covid-19 virus. There is the Centres for Disease Control and Prevention (CDC). It is an American organisation created over seventy years ago. Their purpose is to stop disease coming into America and the spread of diseases. It also goes out into the world to lend its expertise in areas of infectious outbreaks. It also creates laboratories to study the contagion.

There is the World Health Organisation (WHO) a United Nations organisation. Which serves under the banner of promote health for all. It gives it expertise and provides help for all countries that have problems with infectious outbreaks. It was founded in 1948 and is a union of nations.

The European Medicines Agency (EMA) helps to protect the health of people and animals within the European union and European economic area. It both helps and monitors the two areas. It helps improve living conditions and distribution of quality drugs.

The UK Health Security Agency (UKHSA) is the UK frontline of ensuring healthy wellbeing against infectious disease and other chemicals. It is empowered in the provinces of England, Scotland, Northern Ireland, Wales.

and Channel Islands.

In China the main body of health protection is the National Health Commission. Which initiates health planning and medicines. It provides the necessities for infectious outbreaks. It provides public healthcare.

In India the National Health Authority (NHA) is the leading healthcare protection in India. It provides assurance of medical care if required.

Africa which for some reason cannot help itself depended a lot on the WHO & CDC when it came to medical aid for virus protection. The continent drained the WHO resources then made big claims on its expertise. The problem in Africa is that many people live rurally and are poor. So there is a problem getting medical professionals. The world is waking up to dire consequences of its actions and cannot see a way out. Where antibiotics are being over used. Diseases without cures are being found.

WHO claim CDC are withholding virus information, with deep suspicion of drug medicines with holding.

Therapeutic

A statement of concern has been how during the covid-19 pandemic scientists on the frontline of the disease infection were threatened and abused while trying to perform their duties. Claims are being made that federal vaccination programs will make better covid-19 vaccine. A new variant called E.U.1.1 has been found in Ohio,U.S. and a new wave of covid-19 is surging in Japan.

The first direct claim that a country did propagate the covid-19 variant as a biological weapon has been directed at China. By one of its own scientists at the Wuhan institute.

As of July 2023 new variants EG.5 known as Eris and XBB.2.3 known as 'Acrux' have started spreading in U.S.A. known as the first post pandemic covid-19 variants. In August EG.5.1 variant found to be spreading in U.K.

Countries around the world are claiming a end to covid-19 restrictions internally and across their boarders. Medical reports are showing a steady controlling ability against outbreaks. Though word is the pandemic is over many people are still dying from the virus. They are saying that the virus has affected the poorest worse. Many countries have been accused of falsifying true extent of infection in their countries. E.g. China, India, El Salvador. Covid-19 considered to be a evolving virus after over three and a half years since the pandemic began.

On 1st / 8 / 2023 Binervax covid-19 vaccine recognised by Medicines and Healthcare Regulatory Agency (MHRA). The ninth vaccine recognised by U.K. Number of infected is rising partly through surges and waning injections. Variant EG.5.1 found to be spreading in U.K. 4722 linages of covid-19 have been found to date. Eris is now beginning to spread around the planet with a sense of days of fever then all your energy is drained away. A new variant called BA.6 and dubbed Pi has been found in Denmark.

Whatever the situation wariness against coming dangers are being depleted by mindless ignorance. It is as if the more protection is suggested the more it is being suggested as not possible. It is clearly a case of trust your instincts and use what protection is at your grasp. Facts of knowledge on how to protect yourself and those around you against contagion are the most important.

Xyclonetize

A virus that is infectious
A airborne pathogen
Vaccine wains after injection
The nightmare that is covid-19.

A pathogen that is contagious
A airborne virus
Vaccine wains after time
The terror which is covid-19.

A pathogen which can kill
A airborne illness that is relentless
A repeated vaccine injection required
The evil what is covid-19.

When infected you could die
A quick spreading airborne virus
A vaccine protection that breaks down
The horror which is Covid-19.

Whichever way you put it , looks like the covid-19 virus is here to stay. Though the pandemic is officially said to be over. There are still outbreaks occurring around the world.
With no permanent cure yet found different types of medication are claiming to be effective against the virus. But there are anxious moments with outbreaks when the seasonal vaccine begin to wane. Booster injections are still being offered, but confidence in vaccine also is wanning.

Scientists claim to have found an animal to human variant. With spread from deer to human.

Is the pathogen just in a lull, then to change and become more viral. Will more vicious outbreaks occur is not known. It is a case of wait and see what happens. Can the persistence of humanity win out. Will the virus burn itself out and fade away. Or does humanity live and suffer waiting for the inevitable. Has human kind the resources and intellect to stop a virus which variants are forever changing in capabilities. Effect or humanities right shall be the answer.

I sense the answer is close, but the answer is to the impossible. As is how many particles are there in nothing to make a single cell. Or what is the dominant when you have the antigens. To which is the adjacent formulating vaccine.

Summary

Since the beginning of historical time there has been mention of devastating diseases causing mass infections.

With the rise of germs, viruses and bacterium. Thus doctors and science stating the next big fight must be against cancer. Where from little known fact to where statements of breakthroughs have been common. Then came the spread of dementia and Alzheimer's disease. Which there is not much know about. But mention of discoveries for prevention.

There is also the infection of HIV and Aids. Transmitted through dirty needles and sex.

The cure just a touch and go situation with the use of antibiotics.

There is concern with the influenza virus, with its prominence getting stronger. Even though there is a yearly vaccine.

Now we have deadly diseases of Covid-19, Ebola and Monkeypox. All with no permanent cure. Just a spin on vaccines and antibiotics. Where there is a waning of resistance against the disease problem. Now with one breath they say it is effectually stopped. Then with the next there is claim of a outbreak somewhere.

With these deadly disease science is not following protocol to find a permanent cure. Thus allowing further provocation of more vaccine and antibiotic resistant variants of infections. With science mitigating the fact that more deadly diseases are coming. Not following drug development protocol for protection that is a certain to happen. There is also the problem of diseases though thought eradicate. Are now on the rise but more resistant to anti-biotics. Considered to be caused by over prescribed drugs by doctors. Disease is only caused by inappropriate protection of the anatomy. Allowing pharmaceutical companies to produce inferior drugs against infection is wrong and also dangerous. Preparation and skill must be more enabled if that is possible. Considering the unknown is a vast expanse of existence. If we do not have protection we cannot prevent and protect. A major outlet for infectious diseases are inappropriate living standards and unavailability of medication. Which allows the disease to spread unabated.